The Darkling Thrush

Josh Lanyon

The Darkling Thrush
Revised edition, April 2012

Cover Art by L.C. Chase

ISBN: 978-1-937909-06-2 (electronic)
ISBN: 978-1-937909-12-3 (print)
Printed in the United States of America

Just Joshin
3053 Rancho Blvd.
Suite 116
Palmdale, CA 93551
www.joshlanyon.com

This is a work of fiction. Any resemblance to persons living or dead is entirely coincidental.

CONTENTS

ACKNOWLEDGMENTS

Thank you for buying this book. It is only because readers like you continue purchase fiction that writers can still afford to write.

~ Josh Lanyon ~

At once a voice arose among
The bleak twigs overhead
In a full-hearted evensong
Of joy illimited;
An aged thrush, frail, gaunt, and small,
In blast-beruffled plume,
Had chosen thus to fling his soul
Upon the growing gloom.

Thomas Hardy, "The Darkling Thrush"

CHAPTER ONE

The letter was addressed to Mr. Colin Bliss.

It sat on my desk, propped against the framed photograph of Antony and me. This reminded me that, as we were no longer "an item," I really needed to dispose of that photograph of my chief and me. It was bound to look a trifle like I was sucking up, and I'd already done enough of that in every conceivable form.

I picked up the cream envelope, studied it. There was no return address, which seemed curious. Brown ink. Another curiosity. Librivenators like myself — in fact, most of the Societas Magicke — used blue. Other branches of the Arcane Services used purple. The general populace favored black. I couldn't think of any particular significance to brown. Perhaps the author simply liked the color. The problem with book hunters is we see a mystery every time pen is set to paper. One of the problems, anyway. I'd heard I had others. In detail from Magister Septimus Marx.

The handwriting was spidery and elegant. Absently I turned the envelope over and tried to peruse it. I can't say I felt any kind of premonition. After all, my kind of trouble would hardly announce itself with heavy stationery and a fine hand. Who handwrote letters in these days of the Varityper? Let alone letters like this one, which offered fleeting impressions of genteel age and sumptuous living: an elderly person…male…an elegant drawing room with heavy velvet drapes, marble-topped chests, and a spread of tarot cards on the table…

I picked up the pearl-handled letter opener and slit the envelope open.

Dear Mr. Bliss,

Allow me to introduce myself. I am Aengus Anstruther, and I have the honor of being the presul of the Museum of the Literary Occult in London. I hope I am not being unduly modest in assuming that you are familiar with our own humble efforts to preserve the written heritage of our metaphysical past...

Amateurs. All too often their helpful efforts were merely a guise for private collectors appropriating magickal texts that more properly belonged in the official libraries. I glanced at the bottom of the note to see if Mr. Anstruther was requesting a donation. He was not. I continued reading.

You, of course, are the gifted author of Secret Societies and Subversive Movements and the discoverer of Sir Florian Botolf's memoirs. Recognizing that we share a certain fascination with lost treasures and written lore, I would very much like to formally make your acquaintance and, perhaps, propose a small but intriguing venture if you will be in town on the afternoon of the 13th of this month. We are having a private showing of the Botolf Grimoire, and I would like to invite you to a viewing here at the museum at two o'clock. If you can attend, please confirm by telecom.

Sincerely,

Aengus Anstruther

The *Botolf Grimoire*. Mr. Anstruther certainly knew with what temptation to bait his hook. Not that I wouldn't have been interested in a peek inside the Museum of the Literary Occult. It was one of several such places I'd hoped to visit when I had first arrived in London eight weeks earlier — before I'd been distracted by other things.

I frowned at the date, double-checked my calendar. The thirteenth was the following day. Not a lot of warning.

Now that I was no longer in favor, taking off for an afternoon might prove problematic — or perhaps not. I had the impression that Antony preferred as much as possible to forget I still existed. It was Basil, Antony's brother and the procurator of Leslie's Lexicons — a front for our local branch of the Imperial Arcane Libraries — who was more likely to pitch a fit if I disappeared for the afternoon when I was supposed to be squirreled away in my cubicle translating and transcribing ancient texts, the least interesting part of the job for me. I liked the hunt.

I studied the number listed and then dialed it on the upright telefon on my desk, confirming shortly after with a curt young woman that I would indeed be available to attend the private showing at the Museum of the Literary Occult. I'd been hoping for such an invitation but had never been able to determine who exactly the presul was over there — not that I confided that to Miss Mildew, nor would she have been interested, as she obviously couldn't wait to get back to organizing paper clips.

Hanging up the telefon, I glanced at Antony's photo again and turned it facedown on the desk. He'd always looked rather supercilious in that picture, although at the time he'd gifted me with it, I hadn't noticed; I'd merely thought he looked like his mind was on important matters.

When I glanced up again, Antony was standing in the doorway — and his expression matched the one I'd just buried in papers.

"Basil seems to feel there's a problem."

Oh jolly.

I asked coolly, "With my work?"

"With your attitude."

Can anything be more awkward than being dumped romantically by one's superior? This is why one avoids office romance if one has half a brain. Too bad for me my little head got what the big head should have.

I said, "I have no attitude, Antony. I'm here to do a job, and I'm doing it to the best of my ability."

"I'm glad to hear that," Antony said, looking anything but glad.

He continued to stand in the doorway and frown at me.

"Was there anything else?"

"No."

I opened Nesta Webber's excellent resource, *Weird Words*, and picked up my pen to make notations on the manuscript before me. I felt Antony watching, but still he said nothing. Tall, lean, handsome in an inbred way like so many of the English aristocracy, Antony had sandy-colored, thinning hair, blue eyes, charmingly crooked teeth. What in the name of All was it about him I found so irresistible, even now when I couldn't stand him?

When he finally turned away without speaking, I felt that inevitable lurch of disappointment. "Antony," I said, and I winced inwardly at the urgency of my tone.

He paused, glancing back. It was not an encouraging look. I said, "I've been invited to a special showing of the *Botolf Grimoire* at the Museum of the Literary Occult tomorrow afternoon. Is it all right if I take off early?"

"*You've* been invited?" He considered this and said at last, "Of course. If you've actually received an invitation, you must go." He hesitated. "I believe Magister Marx is also attending. You might have a word with him. Perhaps you can go together."

"All right." No way on earth was I going anywhere with that arrogant, judgmental bastard Septimus Marx.

Antony left. I rested my forehead in my hand, pretending to stare at the blank pages before me. Two months ago I'd arrived in jolly old England as part of the colonial exchange program between bureaus of the Societas Magicke. And about four and a half minutes after I'd first arrived at Leslie's Lexicons — the dusty and labyrinthine monstrosity that served as the public face of one of the most extraordinary collections of arcane and occult tomes in the empire — I'd met Antony Leslie, the presul.

Antony was charming and handsome and knowledgeable — and I was a long way from home. He took me to dinner, explained and thanked me for the important work we colonials were doing for the society — and mankind — and then he took me back to my hotel and treated me to some of the best sex of my life.

Our affair lasted seven weeks. In addition to being charming, handsome, and knowledgeable, Antony was married. It hadn't seemed like a problem initially. If there was a problem, it was Antony's, right? But seven weeks later, seduced and abandoned (as they used to say in ye good old days) and having managed to thoroughly isolate myself from my colleagues, I began to understand that it was my problem too, and I had displayed some staggeringly awful judgment. Not least in falling for a man who wore ties as wide as Antony's.

So I really didn't need Septimus Marx looking down his long and arrogant nose at me or curling his thin mouth in one of those sneering smiles because he'd turned out to be absolutely right about...well, pretty much everything.

Marx also worked at Leslie's Lexicons, although I was never quite sure at what. He was a magister, a master of some field of study within the Societas Magicke, the branch of the Arcane Services that dealt with written magick. I suspected he was one of the dreaded Vox Pessimires, one of those taxed with the terrible job of destroying those magickal texts too dangerous or powerful to remain in circulation — or even on the shelves of the Imperial Arcane Libraries. Even if it was true, no one would admit it. The identities of the Vox Pessimires were protected. Perhaps it was a necessary job, but most of us within the Societas Magicke found it despicable.

Which was probably why I was willing to believe it of him. Marx was often "in the field." Although in his case, being in the field seemed to encompass everything from conferring with black-market booksellers to retrieving stranded colleagues — which is how we happened to meet the day I arrived on English soil. Marx picked me up at the aeroport. He had been unimpressed then, and he was — if possible — less impressed now.

And I tended to agree with him.

* * * * *

The Museum of the Literary Occult was located opposite Telescope House on Great Lowden Street. It was a grand-looking building in the classical style. Lots of fluted columns and sculptured friezes. It looked like the headquarters for the Imperial Arcane Libraries should have looked. It was certainly much grander than Leslie's Lexicons, and in fact, it was one of the largest private collections of magickal and occult texts in the world.

According to my pocket watch, it was a few minutes to two. I was greeted by a very young, very pretty male secretary in a green velvet suit who led me straight upstairs to what I guessed was the presul's inner sanctum.

"Are the other guests downstairs?" I inquired.

"Oh, the viewing is not until three."

I puzzled this over as he tapped discreetly on a mahogany door behind an enormous embroidered tapestry of Calistra's *Enchantment of the Infidels*.

A voice bade us enter. The secretary gripped the ring of twisted brass and pushed open the door. He stepped to the side. I went past him into a large office. I had a quick impression of long black velvet drapes, wallpaper of gold watered silk, and bookshelves behind leaded glass.

A very large woman sat before a very large desk. The desk was highly polished; the woman was not. She looked like she'd blown in on a hard wind. Her salt-and-pepper hair stood up in tufts, her blue silk suit looked slightly crooked, and her red lipstick was outside the lines of her wide mouth. Her smile of welcome seemed too bright in the muted light of the office.

"Mr. Bliss," she said. The beauty of her voice, a honeyed contralto, was unexpected. "How wonderful of you to come on such short notice."

Behind the desk sat a small, plump elderly man. He was quite bald and resembled a very old baby — though there was nothing youthful in his glittering black eyes. He surveyed me measuringly, unsmilingly. He did not rise and did not offer his hand.

"I'm Lady Margaret Lavenham," the woman said. "I am the museum procurator. This is Mr. Anstruther, our presul."

"How do you do," I said politely.

Anstruther nodded. "Sit down, Mr. Bliss."

I took a spindly chair across from Lady Lavenham.

"I thought you would be older," Anstruther said.

"I'm twenty-three."

"Twenty-three!"

"I've been book hunting for three years."

"Three years is a great deal of book-hunting experience," Lady Lavenham commented.

Anstruther said, "When you get to be my age, twenty-three is very young." He continued to eye me.

I knew only too well what he saw. It was a source of irritation to me that I looked quite a bit younger than my age, being small and slender with wide blue eyes and a mop of strawberry blond curls. I'd tried growing a beard at one time, but the result wasn't worth the crumb catching.

"Tea, I think," the Lavenham woman said. She was speaking to the small brownie sitting at the very top of the red lacquered chinoiserie cabinet in the corner.

The brownie brightened and disappeared in a flash.

A few moments later the door flew open, and the pretty secretary returned with a laden tea tray. Lady Lavenham served hot, flower-scented tea in blue and white china cups.

"No biscuits?" Mr. Anstruther objected, scowling at the tray.

"There are the little cakes you like. The ones with the slivered almonds."

"But no biscuits?"

"No. I'm afraid not."

Mr. Anstruther expelled an exasperated breath. "Do you like biscuits with your tea, Mr. Bliss?"

"When they're available."

"There is no reason biscuits can't always be available." Anstruther gave Lady Lavenham a pointed look. She smiled apologetically at me.

"Next time we'll certainly have biscuits."

"This is fine," I said. "The cakes are lovely."

No one replied. We sipped our tea, nibbled our cakes. I glanced surreptitiously at the marble clock on the carved bookshelf and wondered what I was doing there.

At last Mr. Anstruther took one final slurp of his tea, rattled the cup back in the saucer, and said, "Mr. Bliss, have you heard of *Faileas a' Chlaidheimh*?"

"*The Sword's Shadow*? Yes. Of course. According to legend, it was the great grimoire of the witches of the Western Isles."

"That is not merely a legend."

I opened my mouth, but it occurred to me that arguing with Mr. Anstruther would not be useful.

"It is *not* a legend," he repeated. "The grimoire exists, and we want you to find it."

CHAPTER TWO

"Oh?" I managed to make the syllable polite — which wasn't my first instinct.

Anstruther said firmly, "Mr. Bliss, you have a knack for finding lost things, as your discovery of the Botolf memoirs proves."

I stared at the tea tray. The brownie was back and busily sweeping up sugar spilled from the bowl. I said, "There's no record of the *Faileas a' Chlaidheimh* in the imperial library's archives."

"We all know that doesn't mean anything," Lady Margaret interjected. "It's only in the last fifty years that there has been any serious effort to organize the archives. They were in chaos for nearly a century."

That was true, unfortunately.

"If *The Sword's Shadow* did exist, it might have been destroyed by the church or the Vox Pessimires. It would be nearly six centuries old."

"There are far more ancient texts in the archives."

"Yes, but they are *in* the archives. It's hard to imagine a text as famous and...potentially powerful as *The Sword's Shadow* floating around loose for all these years."

The whole thing was preposterous, and yet...and yet...what if it were true?

Anstruther said in the irascible way he said most things, "I needn't tell you, I suppose, how important the recovery and preservation of this work is. The *Faileas a' Chlaidheimh* carries a significance that is both political and cultural."

Old Magick. That's what he meant. Old Magick was out of favor these days. It was wild and unpredictable and politically incorrect. It could not be controlled or regulated like New Magick.

"I suppose so." I hedged, "Which is another argument in favor of its having been destroyed long ago."

Lady Lavenham said, "Don't say such things. I implore you."

"Well, but we have to be realistic."

Anstruther pushed away from the desk, and I saw that he was sitting in an ornate bath chair. I'd never seen anything quite like it. It was like a miniature gold throne on wheels. He pounded his small, gnarled hands on the arms of his chariot and railed, "No, we need not! Realism is the bastion of the plebeian mind."

I had no idea what to say to that. I chewed politely.

Lady Lavenham refilled my teacup. "It's most likely that the grimoire would have been treasured, protected not only for its religious significance but for its commercial value."

"'Its cover made of beaten gold as thin as paper and inlaid with mother-of-pearl and cairngorms plucked from the bowels of the purple mountains.'" The presul was quoting, but from what source, I had no idea.

"But it's five hundred years missing."

Lady Lavenham corrected, "Five hundred and seventy-two to be exact, but what are years in the lifetime of an idea?"

I suppose I agreed with her, although even then it occurred to me it would depend on the idea.

Anstruther fastened me with his glittery jet gaze. "Do you know the story of the *Faileas a' Chlaidheimh*? In detail, that is?"

"Not in detail, no."

Lady Lavenham said comfortably, "It's one of those folktales that we all know in part if not all."

"Allow me to refresh your memory." Anstruther pushed away his plate with the offending cakes. "I don't suppose, as a colonial, you're up on your fourteenth-century Scottish history?"

It was dispiriting how often I'd run into this attitude. As though, because I'd been born across the Great Big Sea, I was ignorant of the basic history that would be essential for anyone in my field. Even those not remotely affiliated with the Societas Magicke generally knew about Hamish MacAulay and his invention of the mechanical printing press in 1414. His major work, *The Nature of the Tarock*, was celebrated for both its technical and aesthetic attributes, and Scotland was acknowledged by most as the birthplace of modern publishing.

I said, "I know that in the mid-fourteenth century, Scotland was ruled by Donnie Large, the so-called Teacher King, and that it was under his reign that the Western Isles were finally claimed as part of his mainland kingdom."

He nodded grudgingly. "Correct. Limnu, or the Heather Isle, had been held for centuries by the Sea Raiders. It was considered part of the kingdom of Sodreys. Crovan Worm, the youngest son of Godred Worheld, was given the Western Isles after Worheld's death, probably to keep him from contesting with his older brothers for the throne. According to legend, the grimoire was the work of Imohair Moray, the son of the pirate queen Aylth Moray."

This was the part of the legend everyone knew. "The boy was given as a hostage to Crovan Worm to ensure the pirate queen kept her part of their truce. He became a great favorite of the Sodreys chieftain and eventually ended up choosing to die with him in battle against Donnie Large."

"Yes, yes." Anstruther was rubbing his hands in glee. I was unclear whether what had prompted it was the idea of dying in battle or the fact that I knew even this much of the story. "What no one could predict was that the boy, Imohair, would turn out to be a powerful witch. The grimoire he put together was a collection of the ancient spells he collected from the Sea Raiders and from the Scottish islanders, as well as his own original incantations."

This was the idea that most excited those of us in the Societas Magicke: primary spells. Original magick.

Lady Lavenham said in that attractive, low voice, "If the stories are true, the *Faileas a' Chlaidheimh* would be one of the greatest and most powerful collections of spells, rituals, and enchantments ever known."

"That's a big *if.*" Against my will, I was getting excited, though. Their certainty was contagious.

"This is the part of the story you may not know," Anstruther said. "After the Battle of the Standing Stones, the grimoire disappeared for fifty years."

"Fifty years? Only?"

He smiled. I could see why he had got out of the habit. His teeth were ringed in black. Pretty ghastly. "Exactly. Despite what you've heard — or haven't heard — it resurfaced fifty years later in the possession of a mainland conjurer and alchemist by the name of Ivan Mago."

"A fraud and a fakir." Lady Lavenham sniffed.

"Very likely. By then the Long Island was under the rule of Agro Urquhart, a chieftain handpicked by Donnie Large. Urquhart's lady arranged to purchase the grimoire from Ivan Mago. But Mago was murdered after he reached the island, and the grimoire disappeared."

"They were waiting for him," Lady Lavenham said.

Anstruther said, "One version of the story goes that Mago tried to double-cross her ladyship. Pull a fast one. She didn't take kindly to it."

Lady Lavenham was shaking her head. "Even today, most of the island's population centers around the city of Steering Bay. There are long, deserted stretches of coast. Urquhart's castle was on the northernmost point of the island. To get there, Mago had to pass through some of the wildest, most desolate terrain. Most people believe that bandits lay in wait for him, murdered him, and stole the book."

"No one has heard of the *Faileas a' Chlaidheimh* since?"

"No." That was Lady Lavenham. Anstruther clearly hated to concede this obvious fact.

Myth and legend. The book did not exist, according to the Imperial Arcane Libraries, and yet these two were curators of some of the finest and most famous arcane works in the world. Works that the Societas Magicke would kill — well, perhaps not literally — to get its hands on. They were convinced the grimoire existed; I could see it in the shine of their eyes, the barely suppressed excitement of their voices. They believed — they *knew*.

How? Was it merely book fever? Perhaps.

I said, "Is the story that Mago was attacked for the grimoire? Or was the book merely a casualty of bandits?" If the latter, it was surely lost for good: dismantled for its precious gems and gold boards.

"We don't know," Lady Lavenham said.

Anstruther said, "They were after the grimoire."

"The body was horribly mutilated." Lady Lavenham took a sip of tea. "They might have been searching for something or merely exhibiting spleen."

"They wouldn't need to search hard. It's not like he could swallow the grimoire and produce it at a later date. It must have been a fairly good-sized book," I pointed out.

"True."

"Could the grimoire have been handed off to someone else before Mago was attacked?"

"It's deserted countryside, but it's not impossible. There are a few crofts along the way. A few fishing huts."

Anstruther had said nothing for several minutes now. I studied his face.

"Is the landscape such that Mago could have hidden the book in the scuffle?"

He said drily, "As there is no actual record of the scuffle — only anecdotal accounts of the bloody aftermath, it's difficult to say. He may have had time to hide the grimoire. Or it might have been taken by his murderers."

If Mago's attackers had been after the grimoire, it was safe to assume the area would have been gone over with a fine-tooth comb — assuming Mago had had time to hide the book. That was quite an assumption.

"Why did they mutilate the body?" I asked.

Lady Lavenham and Mr. Anstruther looked at each other. She shook her head to signify no knowledge. He said nothing.

For a few moments we didn't speak. I think we were all considering the violent past we had dismissed with academic detachment. The shadow of that bloody history seemed to cast a strange pall over the room with its gleaming walls and velvet draperies.

Anstruther broke the spell. Leaning forward, he asked, “Well, Mr. Bliss? Will you accept our proposition? Will you go to the Western Isles and try to locate the *Faileas a’ Chlaidheimh*?”

His eyes shone. I wasn’t sure what to say. The idea did appeal to me; I couldn’t deny it. It was the kind of thing guaranteed to stimulate my imagination — the imagination of any librivenator. But the odds of success were astronomical. Where would I *begin* such a task? Digging in the sand on the deserted beach where Mago had died?

Granted, the search might serve as material for an article in one of the Societas Magicke’s journals — or even a second book of my own.

And there was no question I was eager to grab any excuse to escape being around Antony for the next week or so.

“You could take a holiday perhaps?” Anstruther suggested. “A short leave of absence?”

“It’s possible I could take a week or two of personal leave,” I agreed slowly. I did have considerable leave stored up. I’d been hoarding it for my stay in England. I had been sure I would want to explore — though I hadn’t considered exploring quite this far.

“Excellent!”

I added hastily, “It’s unlikely I would make much progress in such a short amount of time. And I’d have to get permission from my employer.” Come to think of it, I’d need permission from both Basil and Antony. However, I suspected Leslie’s Lexicons could do quite well without me for a week or two. “I do have other projects due but —”

“We would pay you of course,” Anstruther interrupted eagerly.

I looked at him in surprise. “Pay me?”

“Certainly. Naturally we intend to pay for your time.”

I hadn’t even considered the possibility. That did make it all more feasible…

And less. Belatedly it occurred to me there was a conflict of interest here. If the *Faileas a’ Chlaidheimh* did exist, my efforts to retrieve it should be on behalf of the Imperial Arcane Libraries, not for a private collection. Even one as famous as the Museum of the Literary Occult.

“It’s something I need to think about,” I said reluctantly. “I can’t decide like this, on the spot.”

“Of course you can. You want to do it; why shouldn’t you?” Anstruther added shrewdly, “We’ll pay all your expenses: travel and research, and provide you with a bit of spending money.” He named a sum, and I nearly dropped my teacup.

If it sounds too good to be true, it generally is. But at least it seemed unlikely I would lose money on the deal, and I could always use a bit of extra income. I couldn’t pretend that this wasn’t an extremely intriguing proposition — made more appealing by the thought of not having to face Antony’s pained expression every morning.

I said feebly, “But suppose I’m not successful — which, in all likelihood, I won’t be.”

"We'll get our money's worth," Lady Lavenham said. Her tone was pleasant enough, although the words seemed a trifle ominous.

Anstruther said, "Don't underestimate the durability of antiquities to escape the ravages of time. Glass, metals, even papers have lasted thousands of years. And as we three know, magickal artifacts are especially enduring."

He had a point. Even the most fragile thing of all things survived: bones, tissue, hair…human remains. I turned my thoughts away from grotesque recollections of graves and tombs.

Lady Lavenham put in, "The *Faileas a' Chlaidheimh* could certainly have survived under the right circumstances."

They gazed expectantly at me, and I could feel the tension behind the polite and inquiring expressions. They wanted this very much. Too much?

I took a deep breath. "All right. I'll do it."

CHAPTER THREE

The sun had slipped beneath low cloud cover. The peppery vapor of summer rain mingled with the scent of passing automobiles as I started down the long pyramid of stairs. I happened to glance up out of my preoccupied thoughts and recognized — without pleasure — the tall, thin figure coming my way.

Septimus Marx.

He must have noticed me before I did him, for his light green gaze was fixed upon my face.

"Bliss."

"Marx," I returned, continuing past him.

I was surprised when he stopped long enough to say, "I take it you've already seen everything you wished to?"

"What?" I stopped two steps down from him.

He was already taller than I; positioned as we were, he seemed to tower. He was thin — sinewy, though, not spindly. In fact, he always gave an impression of barely contained force. His black hair was shoulder length in the affected fashion of the English Societas Magicke, his eyebrows oddly slanted in two slashes that gave his face an exotic, almost puppetlike aspect. His eyes were a very pale shade of green like celadon.

He said in that snooty, studied tone, "It's four minutes past the hour. Was the exhibition not to your taste?"

I'd completely forgotten my official reason for visiting the museum was to see the Botolf Grimoire.

My face must have given me away, because Marx's eyes narrowed. I said the first idiotic thing that popped into my head. "I just remembered I left the stove on in my flat."

Well, it wasn't that bad. It might have even been true; I did frequently forget to turn the stove off and the lights down.

He said, "In that case, as you've probably burned the building down by now, you might as well stay and enjoy the exhibit."

I laughed merrily. "I'll run home and check. I still might be able to hide the evidence of arson." I continued down the stairs, past the big stone griffins, and all the way I could feel the weight of his gaze pinned between my shoulder blades.

Marx already thought I was a waste of space. This would merely confirm it. Not that I cared. Better that than he discover what I was really up to.

As I walked along the street, I considered this. Did I really consider what I was "up to" so wrong? I didn't for one minute imagine I was going to find the *Faileas a' Chlaidheimh*, so there was no question of a genuine conflict of interest between my role as librivenator and using my book-hunter skills for private gain. Not that I wouldn't *try* to find the grimoire. I'd try my damnedest, as a matter of fact, but the odds against it were astronomical. No, this was simply a paid-for holiday at a time when I desperately needed one.

By the time I returned in two or three weeks, the tempest in a teapot caused by my affair with Antony would have blown over. Antony would have started some new romantic intrigue, and the disapproving attention at Leslie's Lexicons would have a fresh focus.

This quest of Lavenham and Anstruther's was a godsend. There was nothing to feel guilty or nervous about — regardless of how it might look to others. However, I wasn't so naive that I couldn't guess how it *would* look to others; I realized I needed to keep my plans a secret, at least for the time being.

Unseeing, I watched couples pass by me, men and women — or women and women — strolling arm in arm. A glimpsed face registered on my consciousness. The woman who had just passed me was someone I had seen earlier. I had a vague impression of delicate blue pallor beneath a sheer white veil, blue-black hair, and dark eyes. I turned around, but the tall, slender figure in gray silk was already rounding the corner.

I hesitated. Had I seen an actual member of the Seelie Court? In London? And at such an unlikely time of day?

The summery rain began to fall harder, and every surface, pavement and awning and automobile, was wet and alive with glistening, glinting rain. Parasols and umbrellas popped open like flowers blooming along the busy street.

I decided that I would go back to my flat after all. No one would be expecting me back at the office, and the idea of running into Septimus Marx again was enough to put me off the idea of returning to the museum to view the Botolf Grimoire, as much as I'd have liked to see it.

Turning, I started back the way I had come, and once again I saw the woman in gray silk walking toward me. I couldn't seem to avert my gaze. She was taller than I, as one would expect from the faery folk, very slender. She wore a stylish tricorn hat with a sheer white veil. Behind the veil, her reddish brown eyes held my own as we once again crossed paths. Now I was sure she was Seelie Court. Despite the gloves and veil, I knew I was not imagining the decidedly blue tint to her complexion.

I looked over my shoulder, but she continued unhurriedly on her way down the street. Even in the colonies we knew that one did not speak to a member of the Seelie Court before being addressed.

Most perplexing. I was still thinking it over as I caught a streetcar and continued on my way home.

I was rooming at a boardinghouse on Tabard Street in the Borough. It was a shabby old place, but clean and relatively quiet. The other boarders were elderly pensioners and students. People in transit. The Societas Magicke kept rooms there for exchange members from foreign bureaus, and I had spent an interesting evening or two lately perusing the books left by my predecessors. The perusal had demonstrated more clearly than anything else could have that my affair with Antony was simply — for him — one in a long, long line.

I was thinking about that, about Antony, as I sat in the window seat and listened to the lonely music of rain gurgling in the storm drains and the hiss of tires on the street below. I had told myself again and again that I was not in love with Antony, but all the same one week, let alone two, seemed to be a very long time to go without so much as a glimpse of him. It was weak and foolish, but…it's not easy to stop, even when you know your feelings aren't returned.

For many, many reasons it would be a good idea for me to take a holiday now.

But the more I tried to reassure myself what good sense this journey made, the more uneasy I became. Perhaps it had to do with seeing the faery woman. Could it be a coincidence that upon accepting the task of hunting for a famous Scottish grimoire, I should see a member of the Scottish fey folk? Was it an omen? And if so, was it ill or good?

After batting the idea back and forth, I went downstairs and quietly telefoned the Museum of the Literary Occult and asked for Mr. Anstruther.

It seemed quite a time before he got on the line and I remembered, belatedly, that he would still be in the middle of the private showing of the Botolf Grimoire.

"Yes, Mr. Bliss?" he asked at last, impatiently.

"I apologize for disturbing you. I need to ask something, though."

"Well?"

"Why me? I mean in particular? Why choose me to try and locate the — *it*?" At the last instant I recognized the danger of speaking the grimoire's name aloud. "There would have to be any number of people better suited to this kind of thing."

"Nonsense. You're ideally suited. Your discovery of the Botolf memoirs…"

He went on talking, but I stopped listening. While it was true that I had, technically, recovered the Botolf memoirs and arranged for their publication, it wasn't quite the impressive story it had seemed in the articles I'd written. Well, that was partly dramatic license. The real story was fairly dull, and who wanted to read about a lonely old woman handing over a box of private papers to her equally lonely young lodger?

I said, when he seemed to be slowing down, "But that wasn't the same kind of thing at all, Mr. Anstruther. For one thing, the Botolf memoirs weren't really lost, only…misplaced. And for another, Botolf has only been dead sixty years. You're asking me to find something that has been missing for nearly six hundred."

"You're backing out?" he demanded harshly.

Was I?

When I didn't answer, he coaxed, "Go to Scotland, Mr. Bliss. Poke around; see what you turn up. Either way you'll have your article or even your next book perhaps — and we will have our curiosity satisfied. And perhaps you will turn up a new lead."

The old man knew the right buttons to press, all right. What scholar of antiquities didn't hope to uncover some long lost artifact? Say it: *treasure.*

"I don't suppose it would hurt to poke around a little," I conceded finally.

"Excellent!" Once again he was all warmth and cordiality. "The fact that someone of your caliber will oversee the adventure will be something — to have our questions at long last answered. Does that make sense?"

Not really, but…oh well, what the devil.

"Very well. If you're sure you want me for this." I prepared to disconnect, but Anstruther said suddenly, "Mr. Bliss!"

I paused at the urgency of his tone. "I'm still here."

"You asked why no one else had been asked to undertake this…quest. The truth of the matter is we did hire someone else. Briefly."

"Who?" I asked with foreboding.

Anstruther sidestepped, saying instead, "You know, there's no danger in this quest, no threat to you, no peril in it at all. It's an academic endeavor that's all. We — Lady Lavenham and I — wish to satisfy our intellectual curiosity. If we believed there was any risk, we would not…fund such a venture. We're not adventurers or treasure hunters, you know."

I withheld comment.

Into my waiting silence, Anstruther admitted, "However, we did interview a few people before you came to our attention with those articles on your discovery of the Botolf memoirs. We knew at once that you were the right person for this job. It requires someone of imagination and…delicacy."

Delicacy? Not something we're often accused of in the colonies.

Anstruther was still talking in that awkward, stilted way. "One of these people was most unsuitable…"

"Unsuitable how?"

"Would you happen to know of a woman named Irania Briggs?"

"I don't think so. Who is she?"

"She's a — It's difficult to know how to describe her."

Never an endorsement.

Anstruther seemed to settle on, "She's an oddball. An eccentric."

Well, it took one to know one.

Before I could interject anything, he added, "I might as well not beat around the bush. She's a villainess. A good old-fashioned adventuress — and crook. They say she murdered her lover, Lord Rockinghill."

"Did she?"

"Probably. It doesn't matter. She knows her stuff."

The stuff, it appeared, that a crook and a murderess would know. I asked, "And she is also now looking for *The Sword's Shadow*?"

"Unfortunately, yes. Don't worry. She doesn't know the second half of the story. She can't know about Ivan Mago and the attempt to purchase the grimoire by Agro Urquhart's lady. As far as she knows, the grimoire disappeared five hundred and seventy- two years ago after the Battle of the Standing Stones. But she has a sort of instinct

— yes, that's the word. An uncanny instinct for the beautiful and rare and powerful."

"Is she *magus*?"

"No. No, a more nonmagickal, earthly creature you couldn't hope to find. She's a book dealer. Mostly old books and rare books, but strictly — at least up until now — non*veneficus*."

"What's her interest in the — it?"

"Lavinia — Lady Lavenham — and I consulted her early on. She has an instinct for these things, as I said, but we quickly realized we needed to bring on someone with an academic background. The original idea was Irania would work with that person."

"So we're working together?"

"No."

"No?"

"Irania has many contacts, many resources, but the more we considered the matter, the more uneasy we became. She's been involved in too many shady transactions. Nothing proved, you understand, but...upon further reflection we realized it would be most unwise to bring in someone with a criminal background."

"I thought nothing was proved?"

"Where there's smoke, there's fire."

"So she's out of it now?"

"Yes. Except...we thought we should warn you."

I repeated carefully, "Warn me?"

"Since she's liable to take an interest."

My stomach dropped. “Does Irania — Miss Briggs — know she’s out of it?”

“Er…no.”

“And when she does know she’s liable to decide to proceed on her own?”

“Er…it’s possible. Not probable, but…we can hardly stop her. It’s not as though we own the rights to *Faileas a’ Chlaidheimh*.” He seemed to run out of words. It took me time to find some of my own.

“And you think she might prove…dangerous?”

“No, no!” Anstruther was practically squawking with alarm. “No, no! Nothing like that.”

All these noes seemed to mean something very different.

“In any case, Irania’s had some legal difficulties recently and is not likely to be traveling. She would have to invite someone in as a partner, and given that she’s most untrusting, most suspicious minded, that’s quite unlikely.”

I had so many questions I wasn’t sure where to start. I could ask for no clearer indication that I needed to withdraw from this project. Yet my uppermost thought was that if this Irania Briggs, with her instinct for the beautiful and rare and powerful, was still concerning herself with this hunt for the *Faileas a’ Chlaidheimh*, it was an indication that it did exist.

And my excitement that the grimoire might be real far outweighed my concern that so might a threat from the mysterious Irania Briggs.

Mr. Anstruther concluded, "So it seems to me, Mr. Bliss, that the sooner you make your traveling arrangements, the better." He put the receiver down with a faint but definite click.

* * * * *

"Marx said you failed to attend the viewing for the Botolf memoirs," Basil said, when I saw him the next morning.

Basil, Antony's younger brother, was the procurator of Leslie's Lexicons and my immediate supervisor. He was my height, a little stocky, with pale blue eyes and sharp features. He looked like a watered-down version of Antony. Less hair, more teeth — and minus the charm.

I said, "I felt unwell."

"That's not what you told Marx."

"No, it's not. I didn't think it was his business why I chose to leave."

This offended Basil, although I knew for a fact he was resentful of Marx's position and equally supercilious attitude. "As a high-ranking officer within the Societas Magicke, Marx is your superior," he said.

"I can't help it if I felt ill. Of course I didn't want to advertise the fact."

Basil continued to eye me suspiciously from behind the barrier of his large and immaculate desk. Basil's office was not the largest, but it was by far the tidiest space at Leslie's Lexicons. A fact he was inordinately, in my opinion, proud of. "I can't think why they invited you in the first place. It's very difficult to get an invitation to the museum's private viewings. All but impossible."

"There's no mystery. They invited me because of the articles I wrote about the Botolf memoirs."

"Yes. The memoirs." Basil gave me a chilly smile. He'd made it clear from our first introduction that he thought my "discovery" of the memoirs was a fluke. And since he was largely right, I resented him in equal measure.

"Was there anything else?" I inquired.

"No. Today you'll be transcribing the text from Professor Paradise's fourth volume."

All at once, I'd had enough. "Basil, I'm not a librireddo. I'm a book hunter. Why am I stuck here doing translations and transcriptions? Why won't you ever send me out in the field?"

Basil actually smiled, as though I had finally fulfilled some expectation by balking. "You're not ready."

"I'm a fully accredited librivenator. I've been successfully book hunting for over three years."

"That was in the colonies. You would never have been accredited here. I'm not absolutely convinced you would qualify as a librireddo, if I may be blunt, but we'll train you to the best of our ability while you're with us."

I straightened. "Are you telling me you're never going to send me out into the field?"

He didn't have to consider his answer. It was obvious to me that he'd been waiting for me to ask so that he could put me in my place once and for all. "Correct. For the year you're with us, you'll train as a librireddo. What you do once you return to your home base is up to you and your superiors." It was clear from his tone he thought my superiors were mad enough to do anything.

There were rumors about this, of course. Rumors of snobbery and bipartisan treatment of colonial exchange officers at the London bureau. But I'd never heard of anyone being told they were unfit for service and being relegated to another position.

"Does Antony know about this?" I asked, and despite everything, my voice wobbled.

"I am in charge of day-to-day operations at the library," Basil said loftily. "But in answer to your question, yes. Of course Antony knows. And concurs."

I would dearly have loved to pop him right in his well-fed, smug, smiling face. I was too angry to think of anything very smart to say and only managed a short, "I see."

"Good. Then as we both have busy days ahead of us…?"

He picked up an envelope addressed in brown ink, and I turned to walk out of his office — and crashed right into someone walking in.

Hard hands closed on my upper arms, which is probably all that kept me from bouncing back into Basil's office on my ass.

Septimus Marx's deep voice said, "Whatever did you forget this time? The lights? The bathwater?"

I tore free, muttered an apology, and kept walking.

Back in my own office, I took a couple of turns around the small room and did my best to cool down. I was so angry that my first thought was to contact my own bureau chief back in Boston. All at once I was fiercely homesick for humble Blackie's Books and my own friends and family. Perhaps I should simply ask to come home? Not everyone was cut out for exchange programs.

But that was probably exactly what Basil wanted: for me to quit, to turn tail and run home.

And if I fled, what about the *Faileas a' Chlaidheimh*?

Yes, what about that?

I sat down at my cluttered desk and stared thoughtfully out the round window at the summer's day. The sweet chestnut trees were in golden bloom, and the heavy fragrance drifted through the open window and cut the dry scent of the fungi spores that seemed to permeate this building — the perfume of old books. As angry and offended as I was that I was not being allowed to do my job as a librivenator, if I gave into those injured feelings and left for home, I'd be passing on the challenge of a lifetime. By which I did not mean translating the prolific Professor Paradise's excruciatingly dull fourth volume.

Whereas before I had felt vaguely uneasy, now the memory of yesterday's strange meeting with the curators of the Museum of the Literary Occult soothed me. I needed to get away from Leslie's Lexicons, and since Basil had basically told me I was worse than useless, he could hardly object to my using some of my accumulated holiday leave.

As I considered the practicalities, my heart stopped jumping in my chest, I stopped shaking, my anger and hurt drained away. Fine. Let them have it their way, then. I had better things to do than sit here transcribing the near-illegible notes of an eighteenth-century illusionist.

Feeling much calmer, I left my office and went downstairs to the main book floor, heading for the history section. I browsed quickly, selected a couple of titles on Scotland, and returned to my desk.

There were a numerous brief entries on Agro Urquhart. He had been a mighty warrior chosen by the Scottish king Donnie Large to rule the wild Western Isles after the Sodreys chieftain had been defeated and killed in battle. There were the usual legends about Urquhart's military exploits. He had proved victorious against the giants of Manx and the rock men of the border. He and a small band of his men had twice eluded the hounds of the Wild Hunt. These stories might have been true, or they might not. It didn't seem to me that magick played much of a role in Urquhart's life. He had encountered the veneficus, of course — who had not? But he was no practitioner and did not even employ a magician by all accounts. In fact, he was viewed as being largely responsible for the rise of the cult of Christianity in the islands.

At least before his marriage.

Two years after he was granted the rule of the Western Isles, he married an island woman who went by the name of Swanhild. Swanhild was no island name — and I could find no surname — so I surmised the woman had been descended from the previous Sodreys landlords. It would be Swanhild who, according to Mr. Anstruther and Lady Lavenham, had arranged for the purchase of the grimoire from the mainland magician Ivan Mago.

Why? Was Swanhild a witch?

There seemed to be no information on her at all, and in fact, it appeared that little more than one year later Urquhart had married again, this time to a young woman from his own mainland clan. This second union had borne two children. The boy had died before manhood. The daughter had married and ruled briefly after Agro Urquhart's death.

What had happened to Swanhild? There was no mention of her death. No mention of her at all beyond the fact that she had married a great warrior — and that she had once, vainly, tried to buy a famous and powerful book of spells. But even that last was not mentioned in the history books. I only had Lady Lavenham's and Mr. Anstruther's word for it.

If I wanted to dig further — investigate how the book might have ended up in the hands of Ivan Mago, for example — I would have to access the records of the Imperial Arcane Libraries, and I was hesitant to do so. Maybe I was paranoid, but I now suspected Basil might be having me watched. Not because he had any inkling of what I was up to, but because, thinking me as inept as he apparently did, he was unlikely to trust me with the most valuable and rare tomes.

Ironically I might have to do my research at the Museum of the Literary Occult.

"You seem to be in a better mood," a familiar voice said from the doorway of my office.

I jerked my head up, hauled without warning back to unpleasant reality. Septimus Marx stood in my doorway.

CHAPTER FOUR

"To what do I owe this honor?" It came out more rudely than I intended, although associating Marx as I did with the humiliating scene in Basil's office, polite words were probably beyond me.

"May I come in?"

I nodded reluctantly.

He took the chair in front of my desk. It was somehow too small for his rawboned height. But then my office seemed too small for him. I could only remember him stopping by once before. That had been the second day after my arrival in England. He had asked me to lunch in that brusque way of his. I'd been relieved that I could honestly say Antony had already invited me. Marx made me nervous — had done so from the moment we'd met, although I couldn't explain why.

Not then, anyway.

I closed the book I had been reading, conscious of his light, curious gaze.

"Basil shared with me your conversation this morning."

"Of course he did."

Marx gave me that narrowed look of his. "Basil could have put it more tactfully, but his reasoning — whether you see it or not — is sound. Three years, even so notable a three years as your own, is still very green in book-hunter terms. And this continent is very different from the Americas. Our written traditions are much older, much more sophisticated, and much more treacherous."

Here it was again: the familiar attitude that the colonies were peopled by savages and that until a few years before we'd all been writing spells with charcoal on cave walls.

"In other words, I'm to be kept tied to home base for my own protection."

"Yes."

I let my not-so-polite disbelief show in my smile.

Marx's face, high boned and haughty, altered with impatience. "You know how short we are of qualified librivenators. Do you honestly believe that we would keep you out of the field in order to win points in some territorial pissing match?"

I did believe it of Basil, absolutely. Of Marx...probably not. That was not to say I believed he was right or justified in his comments, merely that I didn't think it was personal with him. I doubted if anything was ever personal with him.

"Then why was my application for the exchange program accepted? Sitting around here is a waste of my time." I tried to match his reasonable tone, but my frustration came through loud and clear, especially when an impatient wave of my hand nearly knocked over my teacup.

Marx steadied the cup. "That was an oversight. No one bothered to note your age or pay attention to your lack of field experience. We were..."

He didn't complete the thought, and I asked curiously, although I suspected the answer, "You were what?"

"Focused on the fact that you were the discoverer of the Botolf memoirs."

"I see." I sat back in my chair.

Marx added, "You're wrong, though. There is more value to the exchange program than across-the-board job fulfillment. The opportunity to learn and network with a foreign branch of the service is significant. And forgive me, if you were more experienced, you'd realize how significant it is."

"No doubt, but the truth is, I wouldn't have come here if I'd realized I was going to be stuck behind a desk for a year." That probably confirmed his opinion of my lack of maturity, but I couldn't help adding, "Instead of gaining experience in my chosen field, I'm losing further time and training merely so that you and some others could satisfy your curiosity about me."

That hit home.

He said grudgingly, "Perhaps we haven't been completely fair to you. I've told Basil that I'll work with you when I can, take you out in the field as my schedule permits, try to train you in our methods."

It was probably a generous offer, but it was also so condescending, so patronizing, I could barely contain myself. Instead of saying the angry words trembling on my tongue, I said nothing.

My lack of enthusiasm must have been notable. Marx's expression grew uncertain, then wary.

"I'm attempting to help you," he pointed out at last.

"Thank you."

"If you prefer to sit here copying out that tripe, be my guest." He cast a contemptuous glance at Professor Paradise's stacks and stacks of manuscript.

Still, I managed to spew none of the words burning like bile in my throat.

"In return, I'd like something from you," Marx said.

I raised my brows.

"You didn't go to the Museum of the Literary Occult to see the Botolf Grimoire. What were you doing there?"

Unfortunately it was the last straw. I rose. "You'll have to ask them, won't you?" I nodded to the door. "If you'll excuse me, Magister Marx, I've got a lot of tripe to wade through this afternoon."

After Marx left, I brushed the icicles — metaphoric — off my desk and telefoned Mr. Anstruther. I was told he was unavailable, but when I asked for Lady Lavenham, I was put right through. She assured me in that melodious contralto that their museum was mine to use as necessary, and I decided to spend my luncheon on further research — away from the eyes of the Societas Magicke.

The rest of the morning was slow and dull. If Professor Paradise had an original thought, he'd never bothered to write it down. On my noon break, I grabbed my raincoat and umbrella and headed over to the Museum of the Literary Occult.

It was a beautifully appointed place. Marble floors and marble columns gave way to room after room of plush forest green carpets and pale green walls. The bookshelves formed tall mazes of gilt and leather spines.

There were only a few fellow scholars wandering the silent halls with me. Serious little men with pince-nez and tall, grave women in tweedy blazers.

As before, I started my search with Agro Urquhart. In addition to the usual accounts of prowess in battle against the painted hill men and the Sodreys chieftains, I came across the three same legends about the giants of Manx, the rock men of the border, and the hounds of the Wild Hunt. We all have a tendency to attribute great success or failure to outside forces — divine or arcane. There seemed no real touch of the veneficus in Urquhart's life until his marriage. According to a battered text titled *Historical Tales of the Wars of Scotland*, Swanhild Somerhairle was indeed a witch.

Somerhairle. A Gaelic name. An island sire and a Sodreys dam. So a daughter of two worlds.

I tried perusing the book, but I picked up only cadences of other readers…and those long ago: tobacco-stained fingers and garlic sandwiches, a spilled glass of wine — and not the first nor the last — a short stint in a fine manor house library where the book had served as decor rather than instruction, and then Antony. My heart skipped a beat. For an instant I could smell the musky scent of his aftershave, feel the texture of his freckled skin, taste his mouth…

I opened my eyes and focused on the job before me. If this statement regarding Swanhild was fact and not rumor, it did partly answer the question of why she had tried to buy the grimoire from a mainland conjurer. Perhaps I would do better to concentrate my initial investigation on Swanhild rather than her warrior husband.

I didn't get far. Though Swanhild was listed several times in several different volumes of books about the Western Isles, there was no more information than the date of her marriage — 1387 — and the information that she had been a practicing witch.

There was no record of her birth, no record of children born to her, no record of her death, yet I knew from my earlier reading that Urquhart had remarried little over a year after their wedding.

Every book I found carried the same information — or lack of information.

My luncheon break was nearly over. I put the books away, turned to leave when another idea occurred.

I left the reading room and headed down the long corridors to the print room.

My gamble paid off. After listening in silence to my request, the art-room conservator disappeared for a few minutes and returned with a giant scarlet leather portfolio. He leafed expertly through the brittle pages and came at last to a colored sketch, which he placed carefully on the table between us.

"Agro Urquhart."

The man depicted in faded colors was in the prime of life. His proud face seemed too young for the white mane outlining it. His eyes were dark and fierce and so alive they seemed to stare at me across time.

The conservator picked delicately through more pages. "Here we are. The second subject."

It was hardly more than a line drawing of a young woman, and yet something quite rare had been captured, whether through the artist's skill or some quality of the sitter.

"This is Swanhild Somerhairle?"

He double-checked the name at the bottom. "That's what it says."

I understood his caution. Historical records are only as accurate as the people keeping them are careful. I studied the drawing again.

She had been very beautiful. Even I, immune to the charms of women, felt a lump in my throat at that breath-catching loveliness.

Beautiful and very young. No more than seventeen. Probably younger.

Her hair was dark, an unruly mane framing a small, pointed face. Her eyes were large and wide, probably light in color. The features were delicate, almost elfin. Though she was certainly human, perhaps there were more than Sea Raiders in her lineage. There's something to be said for beauty, for that disconcerting coincidence of bone structure and coloring.

The sketch was unsigned. There was a quotation at the bottom.

Ge milis a' mhil, cò dh'imlicheadh o bhàrr dri i.

"Do you know what the translation of this is?"

The conservator glanced at it and shook his head. "It's Gaelic. I know that much."

I jotted the words down and took another look at Swanhild's portrait. It had never occurred to me to try and peruse a picture, but if I'd had more time I would have tried to convince the conservator to let me hold the sketch and attempt a reading. The quotation, most likely by someone who had often seen Swanhild alive and in motion, seemed a point of interest.

A sudden thought occurred to me. "Do you have a print somewhere in the collection of a same-century conjurer by the name of Ivan Mago?

He looked thoughtful. "One moment."

When he returned at last, several minutes later, he was shaking his head regretfully. "No such name exists in the catalogs or even in the catalog of other subjects."

"It was only a thought."

He smiled. "The collection is limited to the veneficus famous or historically significant, you know. The Somerhairle woman is in here because she was married to a great and legendary warrior, not because she claimed to be a witch. At least, not *merely* because she claimed to be a witch. Not every conjurer and occultist warrants a portrait or even a sketch, but you might try the great gallery."

I thanked him and went on to the museum's portrait gallery on the second level. By then I was quite late returning to Leslie's Lexicons, but I was determined to find out what I could.

The assistant to the galley conservator heard my request and said, “We have Urquhart, naturally. Nothing of the lady here. Nor the other gentleman.” Seeing my disappointment, she said, “Our collection is quite small. You might try the main gallery in Lagentium. Did you visit the Print Room?”

“I’ve just been.”

“Of course a portrait must have existed at one time. The sorceress wife of a legendary warrior? Almost certainly a portrait would have been done in the first months of her marriage. But unless the painting had been engraved at some time or another a reproduction created, a print might not exist.”

I knew this already. I thanked her and went to view the portrait of Urquhart.

It had been painted late in his life, perhaps a decade after the sketch I had seen earlier. The face before me was gaunt with age and pain. The sensuous mouth had thinned to a hard line, but the eyes were still bright and ferocious.

It was not a peaceful old age this man was looking forward to. There was no peace in this one’s heart.

When I left the museum, it was nearly two o’clock. I was going to hear about my tardiness from Basil — in triplicate. But since I was going to hear from him whether I returned to Leslie’s Lexicons now or later, I might as well make it later. Having found the sketch of Swanhild and the portraits of Urquhart, I was curious to see the face of Ivan Mago before I left London. I thought it would make the perusing easier if I had some idea of the central players.

I had one last idea. And a long shot at that.

It was no more than a five-minute walk from Cambury to Russell Street and the Corinthian mansion that housed the Imperial Miniature Society. I made it in three.

They had closed for lunch but were once more unlocking their tall, carved doors as I arrived. I showed my card, and I was ushered to the small office of the society secretary.

"I've been waiting for you," the secretary commented after a few minutes of conversation.

"Waiting for me?"

"Yes. Not you, necessarily, but someone like you." I sensed her excitement as I was ceremoniously conducted to the room on the second floor. She left me, and I sat down to wait.

The secretary returned bearing a small square case. "We don't have anything on Urquhart or his lady, *but*" — she set the case upright before me on the table — "this is Ivan Mago."

The miniature had been painted on some kind of a card. I stared in fascination.

"How did you come by it?"

"I don't know, to be honest. No one knows. It's the oldest miniature in the gallery, and until this moment, I thought that was its only claim to fame."

"Are you sure it's him?"

She chuckled and pointed to the small gold engraved plaque at the top of the box. *Ivan Mago*, read the rough script.

"It's quite different from the rest of our collection."

"How so?"

"The presentation for one thing. Have you not yet noticed that the portrait is painted on the back of a tarot card?"

I picked up the case and carefully examined it. Lined with green velvet and framed in ebony, it was not much larger than a paperback. The miniature itself was lacquered in brilliant yellow-brown, tiny fissures of time etched across the striking features.

I asked, "Do you know what card it is? Whether it's from the Major or Minor Arcana?"

"Legend has it that it's the Magician. We would have to destroy the shadow box to know for sure."

"Ah." The Magician would be an obvious choice. The card of creative power and opportunity. And when reversed: power used for sinister ends and failed opportunities.

"The other point of interest is the copper nameplate at the base of the box. Usually these plates were engraved in a flowing, cultured hand."

I caught her meaning. Mago's name was carved in crude, blunt letters.

"Also, most of the miniatures of this era had Latin mottoes and the signature of the miniaturist. Not so in this case."

"What do you think is the significance of that?"

She shook her head slowly. "That despite the skill of the work, the artist is one unknown and unrecognized. Perhaps someone who died early into his career. Or…"

"Or?"

"The work is by an artist known to us, but one who wished his work on this portrait to remain anonymous."

"Do you recognize the work?"

"It could be one of several well-known miniaturists of the era."

The tiny enameled portrait was one of the most arresting I'd ever seen. And yet I was hard-pressed to say why. He was not young — perhaps thirty — and he did not have that smug, self-satisfied look so many subjects of these tiny portraits did. Nor was Mago handsome, not in any conventional sense. His hair was brown, his eyes were blue, but as I stared at his long, angular face, I had such a vivid sense of his character that I felt almost uneasy. Not a man to be trifled with, I thought.

"Who was he?" the secretary asked.

"No one." I clarified, "No one important. Not that we know of. He was supposedly a Scottish conjurer. He died around 1388."

"If I had tuppence for every Scottish conjurer!"

"Too true."

"I'm disappointed. I thought Ivan would surely have a story to tell." She studied the miniature affectionately.

"Perhaps he has. We just don't know it yet."

Well, now I had seen the three principals in the drama: Ivan Mago, who had mysteriously (according to legend) gained possession of the *Faileas a' Chlaidheimh* after the Battle of the Standing Stones. He had promised to sell the grimoire to Urquhart's lady and had either fallen victim to his own machinations or the machinations of the Urquharts — unless he had been unlucky enough to simply fall foul of bandits. Swanhild Somerhairle, who had wanted the grimoire for reasons unknown and had disappeared or died within the year of Mago's death and the grimoire's disappearance. Agro Urquhart, the legendary warrior, who had remarried within a year of his island bride's death. Three figures shrouded in the mysterious past. If I could solve the mystery of the relationship among these three, perhaps I could discover what had happened to the *Faileas a' Chlaidheimh.*

Or perhaps I would go to the island and find the grimoire misfiled on a bookshelf.

I thanked the secretary and left. A thrush was singing as I stepped outside. A thrush in the middle of London singing its wild woodland notes to the passing traffic. The afternoon sun was on the downward slide, the lilacs lining the pavement, heavy, drooping spires in every shade from delicate pink to deepest purple. I walked through the blue shadows, lost in my thoughts.

CHAPTER FIVE

It seemed a very long time ago Septimus Marx had sat in my office and offered to train me in the English style of book hunting. Usually I would be meeting Antony at a pub or perhaps a hotel lounge where we would have cocktails and then go up to a nicely appointed room where we could give up pretending we had anything to talk about.

Now that my married lover had returned to his wife, this was the worst time of day for me. I needed to stay busy, and this adventure was exactly what I needed.

When I reached the boardinghouse, I walked through the main room to the stairs.

"Mr. Bliss?"

Turning, I saw a small, slender woman sat in the parlor. She wore simple but expensively tailored dark clothes. Her pale hair was pulled severely from her face. She looked like a nun or a religiosi, and yet…

"Yes?"

She smiled. The smile transformed her face. All at once I saw that she was quite beautiful. Far more beautiful than the obviously lovely or those who dressed to flatter their attributes. She said, "I'd hoped to catch you at the bookstore, but you had left for the day."

"Yes, I had some errands to run."

"Yes, so I heard." She rose and offered her gloved hand. "My name is Irania Briggs."

Somehow I wasn't surprised. "How do you do?" I took her gloved hand briefly.

"I hope you don't mind my dropping by like this unannounced?"

"No." I was wondering how she got my address. The Societas Magicke was strict about that kind of thing. Had she followed me?

"I know it's unusual, but this is rather urgent. Your landlady, Mrs. Potter, gave me permission to wait, so I took the liberty. Might we go upstairs and speak in private?"

I replied awkwardly, "I don't know. Mrs. Potter is fairly strict about that kind of thing."

Irania Briggs smiled again, and I knew how ridiculous I sounded to a woman with her history — even the much-abbreviated version of it that I'd heard. I wondered how the devil she'd discovered my involvement in the search for the *Faileas a' Chlaidheimh* so quickly. I'd only met with Anstruther and Lavenham the day before, yet here she was on my very doorstep. I couldn't believe that either of those two had revealed anything; Anstruther had specifically warned me against revealing any details of my participation in their scheme.

She was still chatting. "Oh, I promise to behave myself. Really this won't take long. Only a few minutes of your valuable time."

The amiable mockery in her tone decided me. I led the way upstairs and let her into my flat.

She didn't look around, which was as well, since the room was its usual disordered jumble of books and teacups and notes. Nor did she make any attempt at polite conversation. As the door closed behind us, she said briskly, "You've been engaged by the presul of the Museum of the Literary Occult to hunt for *The Sword's Shadow*, yes?"

I couldn't see a point in lying. She obviously had an informant — and a well-placed one at that. "Yes."

She relaxed slightly. "Mr. Bliss, I don't know if you're aware that Mr. Anstruther and that woman had already spoken to me, committed to me. We met on several occasions. They'd actually given me the go-ahead to find a partner in this quest, and when I'd lined someone up, they told me they had changed their minds, given up the entire idea. Obviously a lie."

"I'm sorry. They did tell me they'd spoken with you, but they made it very clear that whether I took this on or not, they would not be doing business with you."

"Did they tell you why?"

"They alluded to…certain incidents."

She was silent. "I see," she said at last.

"I am sorry," I said again, awkwardly.

Her eyes, a very light brown color like toffee, flashed to mine. "Well, it's business of course, and I don't take it personally. It's disappointing, granted."

"I suppose so."

"However, if you *are* sorry, then perhaps you'll do me a favor."

"Perhaps," I said guardedly.

"I'd like to join you in this quest."

Whatever I had expected, it wasn't that.

Before I could respond, she added, "I know what you're thinking, but this is my area of expertise after all."

Treasure hunting was what she meant, surely? What kind of area of expertise was that? "I…don't think so, Miss Briggs. I appreciate the offer, but I'm quite sure my employers would not be in favor of such an arrangement."

She gave me that engaging smile again. "They don't need to know."

I laughed too; I couldn't help it. She was very engaging. "I couldn't work like that."

"Are you *so* honest, then? So sincere and aboveboard in all your dealings?"

That tone and the glint of derision in her eyes were less engaging.

I said, "Let's be candid. We're competitors in this. How could we work together?"

"But we're not, Mr. Bliss. Your interest is academic. Mine, somewhat different. Together we'd have a much greater chance of success."

"No."

"Why not?"

"Because if this thing exists, it must be safely contained in the Imperial Arcane Libraries — or at the least, one of the most secure private collections. It can't be left loose to fall into the wrong hands."

"Stuff and nonsense." She was still smiling, but I could see she was angry, and something in her anger made me wary. She seemed dangerous — though I might have thought so because I had been predisposed by Anstruther.

"What an arrogant young man you are. Don't you realize you need my help? You have no idea what you're committing to. Who are you? A nobody from nowhere who once wrote a book that no one but these dusty old professors have read?"

"I'm the person the presul of the Museum of the Literary Occult hired for the job."

"That was the old fool's first mistake."

"We'll see."

"Oh yes. We will indeed." She stared at me for a long moment, and then she walked without haste or drama from the room. She closed the door quietly, firmly behind her. It was somehow far more unsettling than if she'd slammed it or stormed from the room.

I went to the window and stared down. In a minute or two I saw her walking down the steps. She still seemed unhurried, confident. I watched her stride off down the street.

Even after she had disappeared from sight, I watched the street below, wondering. Who could have told her about me?

* * * * *

The next day I went to see Basil in his office. Septimus Marx was with him, but when I asked to speak to Basil, he excused himself. I felt his gaze upon my face as he moved past me.

"Well?" Basil asked brusquely as the door closed behind Marx. He was having his morning coffee and fruitcake. Every morning at nine o'clock exactly it was the same ritual. Rich cakes from the bakery across the square and coffee with two lumps of sugar and an inch of cream. He was a creature of habit, Basil.

As was Antony, although Antony's habits were different.

"Since you've made it clear you can easily dispense with my services, would it be all right if I took some personal leave?"

Basil paused in the midst of mopping up spilled tea. "Why?"

"Because the main reason I came to this country was to explore it, and that's not happening cloistered here in the library. Since you don't want to use me as a book hunter, I'd like to do some sightseeing. I have nearly eight weeks of personal leave saved up."

"That might be, but it's rather irregular to use it while on an exchange assignment."

"Maybe so," I admitted. "But I'm within my rights to make this request."

His mouth tightened. What an unhappy mix of contradictions Basil was. He didn't want me to work at the library, but he resented the idea that I might take time off to enjoy myself. Or maybe that was simply the way of bureaucrats the world over.

"I'm aware of the policies regarding personal leave." He seemed to struggle inwardly before saying, "It's very inconvenient, but I can allow you to take one week."

"Two."

Basil glared at me. I stared back. I'd be lying if I didn't admit to some vindictive pleasure in insisting on my rights in this matter. I hoped my absence *would* be very inconvenient for Basil — as unlikely as that was.

His fingers drummed an impatient tattoo on his desk. "Very well. Two weeks. But leave detailed information on your itinerary so we can call you back if necessary."

What an officious prick he was. "Of course," I lied.

He gestured impatiently for me to leave his office.

I was smiling as I stepped outside — only to confront Antony.

"Trouble?" He looked from me to Basil's closed door.

"Not for me," I said cheekily. I felt greatly relieved at the idea of getting away for a few days — nothing whatsoever to do with book hunting.

His frown deepened. "I hope you're not taking advantage of our...friendship, Colin."

My pleasure and relief at escaping the confines of Leslie's Lexicons for even a fortnight disappeared in a surge of angry hurt. I might be a number of things, but I'd never traded on my relationship with Antony nor expected special favors.

"Do we have a friendship?" I meant it to sound sarcastic, but my tone was bitter and too revealing.

"Of course." I don't think I imagined the uncomfortable expression that fleeted across his angular face.

"Don't worry. I haven't done anything to embarrass you or the service. I'm actually taking a few days' leave."

"Leave?" He sounded like he'd never heard of such a thing. Maybe it was weirder than I thought to take leave while on an exchange assignment. "Did Basil…?" He caught himself, looking even more uncomfortable than before.

"No. Basil didn't." I nodded politely and scooted past him down the narrow hallway.

"How long will you be gone?" he called after me.

Without turning, I replied, "Two weeks."

He didn't answer. I heard him tapping on Basil's door and Basil's irritable voice bidding him enter.

* * * * *

I was guiltily brushing greasy meat-pie crumbs from page 987 of Professor Paradise's life's work when Septimus Marx rapped on the door frame and — without waiting for an answer — walked into my office.

"What's this nonsense about taking two weeks' personal leave?"

Did these people have nothing more interesting to discuss than me and my holiday plans? "I don't see what's nonsensical about it. I'm entitled to my leave."

"No one takes two weeks' leave on an exchange assignment."

"I suppose I'm too young and inexperienced to know better."

Marx gave me that narrow look — his usual expression with me. His words surprised me. "How is running away supposed to help matters?"

"How is being stuck here in this rabbit's warren with him?" That was more than I'd meant to say, and I could see by Marx's face my slip hadn't gone unnoticed.

He turned to the small oriel window and stared down at the street below. "I have a project you can help me with starting tomorrow."

Unwillingly I asked, "What is it?"

"According to an impeccable source, an encyclopedia of the eleventh-century Unseelie Court has recently been discovered. We'll travel to Scotland by train tomorrow."

If this information were true, it was an astounding find. Such a work, penned when the faery folk were still active in the affairs of men — would add immeasurably to our understanding of Old Magick. And that it should be a work about the Unseelie Court, the least known branch of the fey — certainly the least friendly to humankind.

But that was not the first thing that caught my attention. "Scotland?" I repeated.

"Yes. You said you wanted to see the country."

What a weird coincidence. Or was it? I studied Marx's austere profile, but it was as enigmatic as ever. "Magister Marx, I know you're trying to be kind, but the fact that you feel you have to arrange field trips for me…" I shook my head. "No. Thank you, but no. I'll take my two weeks' leave, and perhaps when I return, I'll be in a more cooperative state of mind."

Or perhaps I would arrange to transfer back to Boston. I didn't want to look beyond these next two weeks.

Marx threw me an impatient look. "You're being churlish, Bliss. Your feelings have been injured, and instead of —"

"It's more serious than hurt feelings. My professional competence has been called into question. How would you react under the circumstances?"

He didn't respond, and I realized his attention was again entirely focused by something he saw through the window.

"What is it?"

"Excuse me," Marx said and departed.

I stared after him in surprise, then went to the window and peered down. A slender woman stood in the shade of the trees. She made no move to come inside the shop; she simply waited, gazing at the building. There was something familiar about her. I scrutinized her gray silk dress and white veil. Could it be the faery woman I had seen on the street two days earlier?

As I watched, Marx strode out through the bookstore's front doors and approached her. He was either very brave or arrogant beyond belief, for everyone knows you don't approach the fey unless they first indicate their willingness to speak to you.

When Marx was within a foot or so of her, the faery woman seemed to shimmer away to nothingness. Marx stood still.

It was rather nice to see him at a loss for once.

I returned to my desk and waited for him to come back, but he never did, and I immersed myself in the world of Professor Paradise once more. Later I overheard two librireddos discussing the fact that Magister Marx had gone out unexpectedly. They were whispering as people often did when discussing him.

CHAPTER SIX

As the day came at last to a close, I gathered my things, left Professor Paradise's work ready to resume when I returned, and went home.

Mrs. Potter informed me that a letter had come for me in the post. I recognized the spidery brown writing on the fat cream envelope and carried the letter upstairs, wondering if Anstruther had changed his mind.

In the privacy of my room, I slit the envelope, and a check and letter slid out. I picked up the check and swallowed at the amount.

It was too much money. The sum indicated more clearly than anything else could that this quest I had accepted was not an up-and-up endeavor. No doubt the wise thing would be to return the check with my apologies and confess that I'd had second thoughts.

I knew without a doubt that was what Antony would advise. And Septimus Marx too, although there was no reason for me to worry what *he* thought.

Setting the check aside, I scanned the letter. It was prosaic in the extreme. Mr. Anstruther asked that I send reports every other day, urged me to contact him if I ran short of funds, and wished me luck on my quest.

I folded the letter, tucked it back into its envelope, and pocketed the check. It was Mrs. Potter's night to play ambigu, and the lodgers had to fend for themselves. As I went about preparing bread and cheese for my supper, I tried to decide what I should do.

But there was really not so much to decide. I knew what I was going to do.

The following day, Friday, I logged my dreams in my journal, dressed, and went to the bank, where I cashed the check Anstruther had sent. I went next to the railway station to buy my ticket, which I'd been postponing while waiting for it all to fall through. The size of the check encouraged me to book a first-class ticket as though I really were going on a holiday I had saved and scrimped for. It felt like that to some extent.

When I got back to the rooming house, Mrs. Potter told me that I had had a visitor — a tall, blond, well-dressed toff — but he had chosen not to wait.

"Did he leave a name?" The description fit Antony, but it fit thousands of other men as well. Not that I had thousands of men calling on me. Or any.

Mrs. Potter shook her head.

I went upstairs and considered going down to the pub and ringing Antony, but if he hadn't been my caller, I would make an incredible fool of myself — and I'd done more than enough of that lately.

Besides…what was there left to say between us?

It wouldn't take me long to pack. I decided to do some final research. I went to the Hobborle Public Library and read up on the legends surrounding the *Faileas a' Chlaidheimh* itself.

For a book that supposedly did not exist, the grimoire was quite famous. The spells and incantations collected therein were reputed to be some of the oldest known to the Gaels and the Sea Raiders both. Spells that had since been lost to time. Even more exciting from the perspective of…well, almost everyone, was that it contained Original Magick as well — also lost to time. The grimoire was the life's work of a Scottish witch by the name of Imohair Moray. Technically Moray had been the hostage of the last of the Sodreys chieftains, but love blooms in the most unlikely ground. Crovan Worm had fallen in love with his young prisoner of war — and his love had been returned.

Moray had used his magickal arts to keep Worm in power after all the other Sea Raiders had been slain or driven back — used all his skill and power against his own people. And the greatest tool in his arsenal of weapons was held to be the *Faileas a' Chlaidheimh* or *The Sword's Shadow.*

There were many stories about the spells contained within the grimoire's golden boards. Spells that were said to be among the first ever generated. Spells to summon monsters as ancient as the sea itself. Spells, it was rumored, that could even restore life to the dead.

The grimoire was described in lavish detail. Jewel-encrusted boards of beaten gold. Thin as paper, but harder than any targe. It sparkled in the sun like a chalice and burned at night like a star. But there were no likenesses of it in any catalog. There were no quotes from it. Not the smallest fragment of an incantation seemed to have survived.

That might mean the grimoire was only a myth like Calistra's *Enchantment of the Infidels*. Or it might mean the spell book had been completely and thoroughly lost. Or it might mean neither of these things.

On the way back to my flat, I combed the old bookshops along Strand Cross, sorting through dusty volumes of dull correspondence and memoirs and biographies and histories for anything I might use, but other than a very out-of-date guidebook, I found nothing of particular use. I wasn't surprised at my lack of success, given the disappointing resources at both the Imperial Arcane Libraries and the Museum of the Literary Occult, but I was bored, and I didn't relish the idea of sitting around my empty room that evening trying to decide whether I was making a mistake.

I treated myself to fish and chips in a pub and read the evening edition of the newspaper, listening absently to the conversations ebbing and flowing around me. At one point during my meal, I had the feeling that I was being watched. When I glanced casually around, I could see no one paying any special attention to me.

The feeling persisted as I walked back to the boardinghouse, but there was no one behind me each time I checked.

Back at the boardinghouse, Mrs. Potter, in a flutter over how much attention I seemed to be getting these days, informed me I had a telegram.

I tore it open and read the contents several times before the message made sense to me.

SEE DR SPINDRIFT OBAN BEFORE PROCEED LONG ISLAND STOP YOU ARE STUDENT ENGAGED IN SPECIAL STUDIES 14TH CENTURY STOP HAVE WRITTEN HIM ABOUT YOU STOP BE READY FOR INTERVIEW WITH FEW BUT PERTINENT QUESTIONS STOP BRING CHOCOLATES STOP

A. ANSTRUTHER

This was beyond odd.

But what part of this enterprise was not?

* * * * *

In the morning I made careful notes of my dreams. So far they had been unhelpful, but I expected to see a pattern soon emerge. I finished my packing, bade Mrs. Potter good-bye, and set out for the train station at King's Crossing.

The seven-coach train departed at 10:42, as it had done every morning for a century and a half. I watched the station slide by, the people left on the platform waving farewell. After a time I took out my battered old guidebook and read. The book was nearly a century out-of-date, but that wasn't a problem, given that I was searching for something lost far longer than that.

I closed my eyes and lightly perused the book. I picked up an impression of young women…two sharing the book and the journey…sensible shoes and walking sticks…a hiking tour fifty years ago. Before that another journey…a young couple on their honeymoon…seed pearls and lace and a lost shirt stud that led to —

Never mind. Before that...*yes*, a young woman...chestnut hair and freckles...slim square hands on a Varityper...English, but not living in England...a novelist and world traveler married to...a colonial administrator in...not China...not Japan...Burma?

I had her. The author. M.J. Beaton. My book-hunting skills, dormant after being kept cooped up at Leslie's Lexicons for two months, were reviving.

Smiling to myself, I closed the book. Before long I was dozing.

When I woke, I logged my dreams — still nothing there, but I needed to take a closer look — and went to the dining car, which was beautifully decorated with rich mahogany paneling and graceful French antiques upholstered in silver and blue paisley. The tables were elegantly set with china and silver; candles flickered in crystal globes.

With a table to myself, I glanced over my dream log to see if any revelations were percolating. Dreams are the dialogue between the sleeping mind and the waking mind. Often the truth is revealed through this dialogue in a way that simple hard thinking won't bring into the open. Learning to keep accurate dream records was one of the first things we were taught in the Societas Magicke. All branches of the Arcane Services put great stock in dreams.

There were the usual dreams of tripping and falling off rooftops and out of high windows. These had to do with my own insecurities, and I dismissed them. There were also, naturally, dreams of books — always dreams of books. In theory, the book represented everything from wisdom to the need to document my own life —

memories — but in the most practical sense…I was a book hunter. Naturally I dreamed of books, finding books, reading books…or as in this case, being unable to read books. In three of the dreams I could not make out the words in the book I was reading.

There was one other dream, but it was so vague that I had made no real note of it. It was something to do with the sea and the night. Deep within the sea, something was stirring, but in my dream I was uncertain as to whether it was a creature or an underwater storm. Either way, it was too slight an impression to analyze.

I put my notebook aside and ordered cold roast fillet with crème fraîche and mushroom sauce, then selected a wine from the list the steward proffered. It was an expensive meal, an expensive trip, no doubt about it. I would have to be much more frugal once I arrived in Scotland. But as Anstruther had been generous with his funds, I might as well relax and enjoy this part of my holiday.

The steward withdrew, and Septimus Marx sat down across from me.

After a second or two, while I tried to gather my wits, he remarked, "If nothing else, I have the pleasure of seeing you for once speechless."

"What are you doing here?"

"I told you I was traveling by train to Scotland." He had; that was true. Investigating the report of that eleventh-century fey encyclopedia. "Not, I must say," he added, "as luxuriously as you."

"Oh. But I'm on holiday."

"Impersonating a lord, by all appearances."

"As we say in the service, you can't judge a book by its cover."

"Appearances can be deceiving." The steward reappeared with two glasses. Marx raised his brows. I nodded curtly.

The steward splashed a mouthful of wine in my glass. Self-consciously I sampled it. Nodded. The wine was poured. It glowed like rubies in the crystal.

Marx lifted his glass and swallowed a mouthful with apparent appreciation.

I asked suspiciously, "How far are you going?"

"Kilmartin Glen." I wasn't familiar with it. "You?"

I wasn't up on my Highland geography, so I didn't dare lie. "Oban."

"The west coast?" The black V of his eyebrows lifted. "Have you been to Scotland before?"

"No."

The waiter came with my meal, and I picked up my knife and fork, trying not to clang silver on china. The damn man, Marx, made me acutely aware of every move I made — and the fact that most of them were wrong by his standards.

Marx inquired, "What interests you in Oban?"

"I understand the fishing is wonderful this time of year."

He gave me a long look, and I felt color rising in my face.

"What does it matter why I'm traveling to Oban?" I asked irritably. "What concern is it of yours?"

"It concerns me that you're lying about whatever your reason is for traveling."

"It's merely a social lie. It seemed more polite than telling you to mind your own business."

His mouth curled in a derisive smile. "You've been reading up on the legends and history of the Western Isles. Why?"

"I plan to visit the islands on my holiday. I've heard how beautiful they are. And isolated." I put that last pointedly. I could have spared myself the trouble.

"You've never shown any particular interest in the islands or Scotland before now."

I laid down my utensils. "So you've been watching me? Keeping track of the books I checked out at the library?"

"Yes."

"Is that standard procedure?"

"Not for me."

"Then *why*?"

He pulled his pipe out and began to tamp the bowl full of shag. "You intrigue me, Mr. Bliss."

I raised my eyebrows. Sipped my wine. I was angry, but I was even more puzzled — and determined not to show either.

Marx simply observed me. After a moment he said, "You can trust me, you know. I can say without undue modesty, I'm considered to be a good man to have in one's corner."

Undue modesty did not appear to be one of his problems. "If I'm ever cornered, I'll know who to call."

To my surprise, he laughed. He applied a match to the tobacco, drew on the stem, and the first blue cloud materialized. With deliberation, he shook out the match. "Shall I tell you what I believe is going on?"

"No."

He ignored me. "On Tuesday you received a letter from the Museum of the Literary Occult. It was not an invitation to the private viewing for the Botolf Grimoire, because I received my invitation one week earlier, and it came in the usual fashion in the usual-sized envelope. I believe you were summoned by the presul of the museum. Is it still Mr. Anstruther? He keeps a very low profile these days."

I tried to look noncommittal.

My silence didn't seem to bother Marx. "I believe it's still Anstruther. I've not heard of his death, and only death would part him from the presul position. In any case, my theory is that you've been hired to hunt for a book."

I couldn't help it. "What an astonishing idea! *Me* hunt for a book!"

Marx grimaced. "You're angry at what you perceive to be mistreatment at the hands of the London bureau, but you're allowing your temper to blind you to the real danger here."

I stared down at my plate, the meat cooling in the congealing juices. "There is no danger."

"You can't know that." If he had used that superior tone on me or spoke with his usual impatience…but he said it quietly, almost kindly. When I raised my eyes, his gaze was unexpectedly dark with concern.

I opened my mouth, but the words that came out were entirely unexpected. "Are you one of the Vox Pessimires?"

He didn't move a muscle, and yet his face closed, shuttered. "Is that what people say?"

"Yes. You must know it is." It was obvious he wasn't going to answer. "I shouldn't have asked. I apologize."

Still, he said nothing, only contemplated me with that light, unrevealing gaze. I felt a prickle of unease.

"I am Vox Pessimires, yes," he said suddenly, softly. "Is the book you're hunting that dangerous, that subversive or powerful that you fear the interest of the Vox Pessimires?"

I shook my head.

His smile was thin. "You look frightened." He added, "But then, I make you nervous at the best of times."

Heat flooded my face. So much for concealing my reaction to him. It wasn't remotely logical, but I was somehow more aware of him — and had been from the first day I'd met him — than anyone on the planet. Belatedly I tried to analyze what that reaction *was*, why I felt…at bay around Marx. He was not unattractive — not at all, really — although I had always preferred men of Antony's age and physical type. Though older than I, Marx was probably a decade younger than Antony. He was dark and lean and dangerous in a way Antony would never — could never — be.

"I've trusted you with the truth," he interrupted my haring thoughts. "Can't you trust me even this much?"

All at once, I wanted to tell him — at least as much as I could. It was hard having no one to confide in. I was not by nature the taciturn type. "I am hunting a book. It probably doesn't exist. If it does exist, there's one chance in a thousand that I'll find it, so I don't think it's anything that need concern the Vox Pessimires —"

"What is the title?"

I shook my head.

He considered this without comment. "How much are you being paid?"

"Just my expenses and a little spending money. I'm not doing it for the money. I'm doing it because either way, it will make a good subject for my next book — and because I'm sick to death of sitting behind a desk."

"I know why you're doing it."

I thought he probably did, so I told him the rest of the story — naturally leaving out the title of the book and the names of the historical principals. Marx listened, his face going grimmer and grimmer.

When I finished, he said, "Walk away from it."

"Walk away!"

"Walk away," he repeated.

"Why the devil would I walk away?"

"Because it's bloody dangerous. Even more so than I imagined."

"Crazy maybe, but I don't see dangerous. I tell you, the book is unlikely to exist any longer. There's no record of it ever existing in the Imperial Arcane Libraries."

Something flickered in his eyes. If anyone was likely to be able to guess what book I was referring to — and to know whether that book really did exist, it was probably a member of the Vox Pessimires. He said mildly, “Treasure hunts are always dangerous.”

“This isn’t a treasure hunt.”

“Maybe not for you. It is for Lavenham and Anstruther. It is for this Briggs woman.”

He was right about Irania Briggs. No question there. This was definitely a treasure hunt for her. She made no bones about it.

“It’s two weeks of poking around old bookstores and talking to people; that’s all. No one will know or care what I’m up to. I’ll be another tourist.”

“I assume you confided in me because you wanted an objective opinion. Well, I’ve given it to you. Decline. Go home.”

“It’s too late.”

“No, it’s not. Tell them you’ve changed your mind. Tell them you’ve had time to rethink.”

“I’ve spent their money. Part of it anyway.”

“I’ll give you the money to repay them.”

The unexpected generosity took me aback. I didn’t know what to say. “You’re serious.”

“I am utterly serious.”

“Look, Marx, I don’t want to back out. The more I researched this, the more fascinated I became by the whole thing. I want to go. I only told you because you pushed and because…”

“Yes?”

"I suppose I do want insurance," I admitted. "There's always a chance you might be right. As a precaution, it's probably a good idea to tell someone what I'm up to. In case."

"Then you haven't told Antony?"

"No. I'm not talking to Antony these days. And even if I were…" It was ridiculously hard to meet his eyes and admit this, but I couldn't seem to look away. "All right, I suppose the truth is, if I had to back the person most likely to get me out of a jam, you'd get my money. You may not like me — I know you don't — but I know you'd do your damnedest to see I got home safely."

His slanted brows shot up as though I'd genuinely startled him. "Where do you get the idea I don't like you?"

"You haven't made any secret about it."

He lowered his voice. "I don't like your behavior. I don't like the way you're carrying on with a married man — your presul — but I don't dislike you personally."

"It's too fine a distinction for me. And it doesn't matter anyway. Like I said, I know that regardless of your feelings or lack thereof, you take your responsibilities seriously."

"I do." He sounded ironic. "Thank you."

I shrugged.

"Although you haven't given me a great deal to go on if you do vanish off the face of the planet. Can you at least tell me where you're going?"

"You already know. The Western Isles."

"When you're trying to rush to the rescue, it helps to narrow it down between islands."

I hesitated. "If I did need to contact you, is there a number where I could reach you?"

"I expect to be moving around quite a bit."

We seemed to have reached stalemate. I had told him all I was prepared to.

"Do you smoke?" he asked suddenly.

I shook my head.

"I'm getting dire looks from the waiters." He gestured with his pipe. "I'll have to take this to the smoking car. Will you come along?"

I glanced down and was surprised to find a brownie waiting to take my empty plate. It was a waste of a wonderful meal; all my attention had been on the conversation. I nodded in answer to Marx and followed him to the smoking car, where he puffed tranquilly on his pipe, and we both stared out the windows at the fiery sunset, the occasional salient silhouette of a church or castle appearing black against the blood orange skyline. The hills and water turned gold and then brown in the fading light...consumed like parchment in flame.

I stared out the window. "The thing with Antony... I've never done anything like that before. I know what everyone thinks, but I didn't even realize he was married the first night. It didn't occur to me to ask."

Out of the corner of my eye, I could see Marx's face turned my way. I didn't dare meet his gaze. His voice was nonjudgmental. "But you did know shortly after."

"Yes. I knew. I don't have a good explanation for it. I was flattered, and I was lonely, and for some reason it seemed different here than it would at home. I don't know why. I was sick of myself almost at once, but by then…"

By then everyone else was sick of me too. I didn't say that, though. It would sound like I was whinging, and in fact I understood why my colleagues at Leslie's Lexicons didn't want to have anything to do with me.

It was still a lonely position in which to find myself.

I risked a look at Marx. He was studying me in that grave, contemplative way.

Just as I was thinking I'd crack if he didn't say something, he said, "You read too much into people's reticence. And you don't realize how much apart you've kept yourself. It's not a matter of liking or disliking. No one knows you."

"You didn't like me from the moment you first laid eyes on me." In the amber light, his face looked stern and golden — like a funerary mask. It seemed a long time ago, that first meeting. Almost irrelevant.

He spoiled the image by smiling. I wasn't sure I'd ever seen him smile before — not a genuine, friendly smile. "That's not true." Marx sounded amused. "It's quite the opposite. I like you too much."

CHAPTER SEVEN

Something seemed to have been lost in translation. I heard the words, but surely they were open to another interpretation? Despite the smile, Marx's expression was as unreadable as ever.

He appeared to be waiting for me to respond.

"Is that possible?" I asked carefully.

"It could be. If it keeps me from doing my job."

That sounded obscurely ominous. I was reminded that he had admitted to being Vox Pessimires — and no one knew exactly what the full scope of *their* duties were. "Why should it?"

The dusk blurred his features, but there was a feral gleam in Marx's eyes. "Because you're trouble, Mr. Bliss. I recognized it the moment I saw you standing there at Croyden Aeroport with your hair in your eyes and one battered suitcase."

"I like to travel light."

"You like to jump first and ask questions later." The spicy fragrance of his pipe drifted across to me. "Well, that's the nature of the beast. I was the same at your age." He finished with his pipe, dumping the tobacco into the crystal ashtray.

"Are you so much older than I?"

"Old enough."

"For anything in particular?"

He didn't respond. Into that formidable silence I said, awed at my temerity, "Me too."

Neither of us spoke. And then, disconcertingly, the frosted globes of the overhead lights in the coach flared on around us.

It was as though the spell had broken. I winced at the sudden illumination, glanced at Marx waiting to see…well, disapproval, withdrawal. He was watching me intently.

I blinked back at him.

He said, "Did you book a fancy cabin in the sleeping car for this trip?"

"I… Yes. I did."

"I'd like to see it."

Proof of how uncertain I was of both my own intentions and Marx's, I wasn't sure, until the door of my single cabin closed behind us, and Marx turned the lock, whether he was coming along merely to check out the marquetry — and whether that's all I hoped for.

But the lamp came on, lighting the rich wood and creamy linens. Marx moved away from the door.

I had no particular expectation. Antony's lovemaking had been unimaginative but smooth, polished. Well-practiced. I liked that. I liked experience and certainty when blended with old-fashioned chivalry. Most of my lovers were older. Older men appreciated youth — and made allowances for a lack of expertise. Not that I was much lacking in expertise these days, but there had been a time.

Septimus fell upon me like the wolf upon the fold, and it was both alarming and delightful to be ravished with such enthusiastic thoroughness. He tore off my clothes — well, I suppose to be honest, I was a willing accomplice — and by the time I'd kicked off my second sock, Septimus was also naked. He pulled me down on the bunk; his mouth, hot and sweet, seemed to be everywhere at once — the delicious shock of the taste of him — tracing down the curve of my jaw…throat…collarbone… He latched onto a nipple.

The feel of that went through my body like an electric jolt. I arched up, managing to swallow the telltale noises ready to tear out of my throat. "Do that. Yes," I whispered frantically.

As if I needed to give instructions. He read me as easily as I'd have perused a treasured book, and I could feel him smiling at my responses as his tongue flicked my nipples into tight buds. His breath heated my naked skin.

I retained enough presence of mind to offer a few caresses back. It was startling — almost unbelievable — to think that *this* was Septimus Marx. But it felt right. How had I not recognized that awareness of him for what it was? How had I not realized what I really wanted?

Because what I really wanted scared me.

And thrilled me, because it *was* thrilling to hear Septimus say in that rough, deep voice, "I've thought of you every day for the past eight weeks."

"You should have said." I gasped as his mouth transferred to my other nipple.

Simple, uncomplicated sex. What could be better? The incandescent pleasure of touch, of skin on skin, of being stroked and petted and admired — and giving the same back. I could feel myself going up in a blaze of sensation, all the cells of my body sparking and catching light. No wish and no need to think further than these next few moments — even if I'd been capable.

We shifted a little, giving our cocks room to grow — not that they weren't quickly assuming mythic proportions. Septimus's warm mouth traveled to my own. He tasted dark and earthy — a bit like the wine and a bit like his pipe and a lot like himself. My lips yielded to the press of his tongue, and that slick, intimate nudge as he pushed into my mouth brought a moan from me.

Beneath us, the wheels rumbled like thunder down the track, and we moved into that steady, deep rhythm. The stars flashed between the gently swaying curtains overhead.

I couldn't help but distantly wonder what exactly was going on here? Beyond the obvious. Not that I wasn't enjoying myself — there was nothing more enjoyable than the naked friction of one body moving seductively against another, but I had the niggling sense that I was being ever so delicately ushered into this. That there was more than a suspicion of the veneficus in Septimus's expert attentions. But how could that be? No spell was uttered, no gesture made — barring the deliberate movements of his hips rocking against mine. Pleasure quivered through me with the rolling, rocking rhythm of the train. Each sway, each bounce seemed to send flashes through my belly and groin at the contact with smooth, hot skin.

I had enough presence of mind to divert this particular express to a siding, wrapping my hand around the thick weight of Septimus's rigid cock, indicating that this was all I wanted.

It *wasn't* all I wanted, but it seemed safer this way.

"Tell me what you like?" he whispered.

"I like this."

"We can do this..." Septimus responded in kind, and again the meter of his hand tugging on me seemed to match the meter of the wheels undulating along the track. My pulse seemed to match it, slow and deliberate and thick...

Time seemed to lengthen and curl lazily around us. Septimus's body was all muscle and bone and elegant scroll patterns of ink black hair. Starlight burnished him to a landscape of broad planes and subtle dips and powerful sinews. We held each other as the train rocked along, thumping over the rails, locked tight in an interlace of legs and hands and cocks as we thrust our way into the fierce, fraught pulses of release. Hot and sudden and bright.

In the panting, dazed aftermath I waited for him to untangle himself from the damp bedding, waited for him to reassume his mask so I could reassume mine. Septimus reached to tug the feather duvet over us, pulled me back into his arms, settling comfortably into the soft linens. It seemed he was spending the night.

"Sweet dreams."

"And to you," I responded automatically.

In a short while I could feel his ribs moving in the easy rhythm of sleep. His breath was warm against my forehead. I closed my eyes and let myself be lulled by the *clack-clack* and *clickety-click* of the wheels rushing beneath us.

Hours later I opened my eyes.

It took me a second or so to remember that I was on a train, that we would be well over the border by now, that the warm body pressed comfortably against my own was — unbelievably — Magister Marx's. This was all extraordinary, but it wasn't what had woken me.

I turned my head on the pillow, and I saw that someone was staring through the window panel of the cabin door. I lifted my head. I could barely discern the softly luminous face of a woman. Spectral and shining…

The faery woman.

I sat up. It seemed to me that her mouth was moving, but I heard no words and couldn't make out the form of her lips. I looked more closely, started to leave the bunk. Septimus's arm tightened instinctively. He muttered in his sleep. I sank back, still staring.

There was no one there. No one stood on the other side of the door. The shade was pulled down across the window.

I had been dreaming.

* * * * *

Oban was a busy place in August. The hotels were overtaxed with holidaymakers. Tourists seemed to be everywhere, watching boats or listening to the bands playing along the parapetless, unsafe embankment. The bay was crowded with yachts and steamers. The mountains of Mull could be seen in the misty distance.

I took a taxi from the train station. The inn where I was staying overnight was near the harbor. It was small and clean and perfectly suitable — though a far cry from the luxury train accommodations I'd enjoyed on my journey north.

Septimus must have left my cabin right before dawn. I had fallen into a deep sleep by then and never heard him leave. I hadn't seen him again — had made sure of that. I was disquieted by what we had done — as much as I'd enjoyed every minute of it. I had enjoyed hearing Septimus whisper sweet nothings in my ear, but in the cold light of morning I'd had more than a little trouble believing that he had been sincere.

No. I simply did not believe Magister Septimus Marx had been yearning after me ever since my arrival eight weeks earlier. Which meant that there had been a particular purpose behind that expert and ardent lovemaking. In fact, I was convinced I had been expertly seduced — but to what end?

I didn't wait to find out.

Arriving at the inn, I unpacked and had what was described to me as a traditional Scottish breakfast. This consisted of pinhead oatmeal porridge followed by finnan haddock, eggs, and black and white pudding. Between bites — and swallows of tea strong enough to peel the enamel from my teeth — I asked the proprietress if she knew of Dr. Spindrift.

"Och, who doesn't know the guid doctor!"

Well, I didn't, for starters, but it turned out that the eminent Dr. Spindrift was a driving force behind the annual midsummer folk-music concerts for which Oban was justly famous. According to my hostess, Dr. Spindrift was over a hundred years old.

I finished my breakfast while I made belated notes of my dreams — hardly worth writing down, as they mostly had to do with Septimus and carnal reenactments of things we both did and did *not* do — and then I telefoned for another taxi to take me to see Dr. Spindrift.

Dr. Spindrift lived at #1 Strathaven Terrace. It was a small ivy-covered villa on a quiet residential street. I got out, paid the taxi driver, went up the front path, and rang the bell.

A maid opened the door and informed me the doctor was expecting me. She led me to the back of the house through dark rooms that smelled of furniture polish and mustiness and something indefinite — old age, perhaps. We came to a door. She knocked and opened the door, nodding for me to go in.

I found myself in a large bedroom. Despite the warmth of the day, the windows were closed and a fire blazed in the hearth. The room was stifling with slumberous heat. There was a bed carved like a Sodreys boat and a jumble of oversize and fancifully shaped furniture. In an enormous armchair was what appeared to be a little goblin woman. Or maybe a goblin man. It's hard to tell with goblins of an advanced age at first glance.

Or second.

It didn't help that her shrunken body was swaddled in pink blankets. The lacy cap Dr. Spindrift wore over her bald green head covered the tips of her large pointed ears. Her yellow eyes were long lashed and heavy lidded, her teeth filed sharp, as I could see when she smiled a sleepy hello.

Now I understood why I'd been advised to bring chocolates: there is nothing goblins like more. I offered her the box.

She took it with alacrity, a hairy green hand thrusting from the mummy wrap of blankets and retrieving the chocolates. She spoke in a high, childish voice. "My old friend Aengus Anstruzer said you would be paying me a visit, Mr. Bliss. You're a student from ze Americas?"

"That's right. I'm interested in architecture. I was hoping to examine the ruins of Urquhart Castle on the Long Island."

"Urquhart Castle!" Dr. Spindrift seemed excited. "My fazer's great-great grandmozer trained to be zee falconer zere. She was born here on zee mainland, but she traveled to zee islands at zee age of fourteen."

I tried to remember how long goblins typically lived, but Dr. Spindrift was already supplying the information I needed. "It's many years since I've seen zee castle, but I've heard it's still standing. Zere was talk at one time of opening it to tourists. Zee gardens are still zere, I believe."

"Gardens?"

"Oh yes. Zee gardens were famous in zeir day. You must have heard of zem?"

I couldn't remember anything about gardens in my reading, but then I wasn't a student of architecture either.

"Zee garden was still young when my grandmozer came to the island. By zee time she crossed, it was an oasis on zee cliffs above zee ocean. It was a church first, you know. Zee castle."

Something else that had not really registered in my reading, but I did have vague recollection that the castle had been built not far from an abandoned church on the butte of the island.

"I've heard the legends," I offered diplomatically.

"Legends to *you*!"

"True." I watched her tear into the box of candy. "Did your grandmother tell you stories of the castle?"

She — he? — chuckled wickedly. "You don't want to hear about my grandmozer. You want to know about *her*. Of course you do. Everyone who reads of zee castle wants to know about her. Zee sea witch."

Were the stories so well-known? I'd never heard of Swanhild Somerhairle until Mr. Anstruther and Lady Lavenham told me of her role in the disappearance of the *Faileas a' Chlaidheimh*. But perhaps there had been a time when the stories about Swanhild were much more widely known. Especially in this part of the world.

"What was she like?"

"An evil creature! A lovely face wiz a black heart. A devil spirit."

"Where did she come from?"

Spindrift seemed confused by the question. "She grew up on zee island. In one of zee small fishing villages. Agro Urquhart saw her one day gutting fish, and he took her to be his lady in his fine castle. And she repaid his kindness wiz betrayal. Zat one loved no one but herself. Not her good husband or her loving parents. She gave her black heart to a demon prince —"

She paused, panting as though she had to catch her breath. I thought how the bridge of time was spanned by human links. A few long-lived family members could keep a legend alive and current; Spindrift spoke as though her observations were local gossip and still relevant.

"She was well loved, zough. Zat will surprise you."

It did surprise me — although presumably Agro Urquhart had loved her.

"Zat is beauty and charm. It covers a multitude of sins. People like to believe zat beauty is good. She was loved by all but one."

"Who?"

"One of Urquhart's warriors. A warrior maid by zee name of Blair. Only Blair. No one remembers another name. Perhaps she had not one. Her face had been scarred saving zee life of Agro Urquhart from the black hounds of zee Wild Hunt. Zee sea witch mocked her for her scarred face, and Blair, who was a maid beneaz her armor, never forgot nor forgave her."

Interesting, but I didn't see what this Blair had to do with anything. "What happened to her? The sea witch, I mean?"

"She was proud and arrogant. It made her blind to enemies. She did not zink anyone could harm her."

"Why should anyone have wanted to?"

Dr. Spindrift seemed confused. She chewed a chocolate, gazing at me with her long-lashed eyes

I tried another tack. "Was she veneficus?"

The goblin studied me. "She believed she was."

"Did anyone else believe she was?"

Dr. Spindrift chuckled knowingly. "Is zis what you came here to learn? Do you not wish to speak of the garderobes and crenellations?"

I could think of few things I wished less to speak of. "How did the sea witch die?"

"Och! Oh, zere are different stories."

I guessed, "Her demon lover carried her off?"

"Yes! Yes! After she was imprisoned for her treachery and locked in zee sea caves. Zey heard her screaming curses and talking to zee devils, but when zey moved zee rock zat guarded zee sea-cave door, she was gone."

One part of that story stood out for me. "Treachery? What kind of treachery? Did she take a lover?" That generally counted for treachery when one was married. Unless one was married to someone as understanding as Antony's wife.

Dr. Spindrift laughed. "You don't know zee story at all, do you?"

If I did, I'd hardly have been sitting sweltering in that room. I tried to look charming and rueful instead of merely overheated and in a hurry to be on my way. "There isn't much in the, er, architectural texts."

"I don't zink zere would be!" The goblin professor seemed lost in thought; I suspected she'd forgotten I was even there as she gazed into the roaring fire on the hearth. "He must have loved her at one time. But nozing is more bitter zan love turned cold."

Her voice sounded deep and menacing, but when I stared, she blinked sleepily and turned her yellow gaze my way. "Zee ozer story is when zey moved zee rock from zee entrance to zee cave, zey found her body in zee tide pool. She drowned herself."

"Is that what your grandmother said? What did she believe happened? Why did Urquhart turn against her?"

Dr. Spindrift laughed and in the middle of her laughter went to sleep with the suddenness of very old age.

"Dr. Spindrift?" I asked softly.

She began to snore. The box of chocolates slipped out from beneath the blankets and fell to the floor with a muted *thud.*

I hadn't had a chance to ask about the grimoire.

I jumped as the door behind me opened. The maid beckoned to me. "You must leave now. The doctor is very frail. When she sleeps like this, she cannot be disturbed."

"How long will she sleep?"

She shrugged.

Clearly there was no point in waiting. I left the house thinking perhaps I could go back before my boat sailed the next morning.

As I was not so far from the inn, I decided to walk back. I wandered the streets and finally, inevitably, stopped at a small bookshop. Prowling through the dusty bookshelves, I found a small faded purple volume titled *Ancient Island Legends* by Peter Burnham.

I closed my eyes, stroking the worn cloth. Birdseed, pipe tobacco, pencil shavings…hand-drawn maps and wrinkled pages and pages of notes. Now that was remarkable. I'd skipped right past the previous owners of the book and gone straight to the author. Either I was getting stronger at perusing, or the vibrations in this place — or perhaps this book — were stronger than usual.

I opened the weathered boards and flipped through the yellowed pages to a section marked Fatal Courtship. It seemed to be accounts of several folktales or legends about romances gone bad. Very bad indeed.

There was a passage — no more than a paragraph — on Swanhild Somerhairle.

The laird's faithless lady was caught in a trap set by a faithful lieutenant of her husband. Swanhild was summarily executed and buried in the castle chapel.

So it was as I thought. Adultery. I was a bit disappointed by the common sordidness of it. One sentence in particular caught my attention: She was *buried in the castle chapel.*

A simple statement of fact. I read it again and again. *She was buried in the castle chapel.* She would have to be buried somewhere, I suppose. But most of the stories about her had no ending. No description of her fate at all. Dr. Spindrift had offered two legendary possible solutions to the problem of Swanhild. If she had been snatched by the otherworld, she would have had no mortal remains to dispose of, and if she had killed herself, she would not have been buried on consecrated ground. But this was simple enough to verify. Slain for adultery and buried in the chapel.

I took the book to the counter and asked the studious-looking young man if he knew anything about the work or the author.

He picked it up and frowned over it. "Peter Burnham. He wrote a number of these books. I'm afraid the research is rather doubtful."

"Is that so?"

"Mm. Obsessed with Old Magick."

"Ah."

"Naturally he was only interested in stories that supported the existence and relevance of Old Magick."

"I suppose in his day…"

The young man said impatiently, "His kind never change. There are people even today who insist that the only real magick is Old Magick and that New Magick is only a pale and overprocessed imitation."

Yes, and many people of our generation believed Old Magick was unsafe and unsanitary.

"Well, I'll take it anyway. The writing is quite beautiful in parts."

"As you please."

"I don't suppose Burnham is still alive?"

"No. No, he drowned in the Corryvreckan whirlpool back when I was a boy. Looking for more proof of his Old Magick, no doubt. Well, he got more than he bargained for."

I smiled politely and paid for the book.

As I stepped outside the shop, I realized I'd either stayed longer browsing the shelves and old volumes than I had realized — or I'd lost time. As I walked back to the inn, the dying evening sun seemed to cast a tremulous, almost enchanted light over the city. The white buildings glowed rosily, and the glassy water in the bay was opal-tinted wine.

Gulls whirled and cried overhead, seeking scraps. For a moment I stood gazing from the bridge and was surprised to hear the melodious notes of a thrush.

I looked around, but though the warble was distinct, I saw no sign of the bird.

It continued to sing as I watched the great curve of the bay growing bright as the lamps turned on in every house and hotel. Wavering lines of gold traversed the water.

When it was nearly too dark to see, and the thrush had stopped its singing, I continued on to the inn where I was spending the night. I found it crowded and noisy, bustling with guests sitting down to the evening meal.

I sat down by myself at a small table near shuttered windows. A brownie quickly supplied me with cutlery and tableware.

"Forgive my forwardness, Mr. Bliss, but I hope you won't object to my joining you for supper?"

I looked up, startled. Irania Briggs stood beside my table.

I rose and shook the hand she offered. "This is a surprise."

She was demurely clad in blue wool, but her gaze was the direct, glinting one I remembered from our one previous encounter.

Irania seated herself. "It's so dull traveling alone, isn't it?"

"Are you traveling alone?"

"For the moment." She smiled.

I smiled politely back. "I'm surprised to see you so far from London." Floored was more like it.

"Are you? Well, Mr. Bliss, it's a small world, so they tell me."

And getting smaller by the minute.

CHAPTER EIGHT

Was the Briggs woman following me, or had she worked out this much of the puzzle on her own? After all, this wasn't the hard part; it was reasonable that she should have narrowed her quest to the Western Isles — and she wouldn't want to waste time getting here any more than I did.

"What does bring you to Oban?" I inquired.

Irania drawled, "I hear the fishing is marvelous this time of year."

My thoughts had been ticking over swiftly, but at this comment, the internal clockwork halted. I had facetiously mentioned fishing to Septimus Marx the previous evening. Was this a coincidence? Had she been on the train? Irania's eyes glittered mockingly in the candlelight — but then, she always wore that same rallying expression.

"Are you a great fisherwoman?"

She tilted her head thoughtfully. "I'm certainly enthusiastic on my fishing expeditions."

The waitress came, and we ordered our meals. While we waited to be served, Irania Briggs chatted pleasantly about inconsequentials. I smiled politely and silently fretted over what her presence indicated.

When our meals, accompanied by tankards of red ale, were set before us, Irania said abruptly, “Have you had time to rethink my offer, Mr. Bliss?”

“I’ve had time, but I still feel that partnership wouldn’t be in either of our best interests.”

She daintily sipped her ale and replaced the tankard on the table. “I should be offended. I suppose you’ve been listening to gossip. Aengus Anstruther is a fearful old woman, and that other old woman he calls his procurator is worse. The question you should be asking yourself is not why *I* want *The Sword’s Shadow*. I make no bones about that. What you should ask yourself is, why does the Museum of the Literary Occult want it?”

“That’s obvious.”

“Is it? By all accounts it’s a very dangerous book.”

“That could be said of any book. Or of any idea.”

“Old Magick, Mr. Bliss. You know what they say about Old Magick.”

I shrugged.

She said, “It’s a very valuable book.”

“Anstruther is too old and too ill and too rich to worry about *that*.”

This idea seemed to amuse her.

Irked, I said, “Why does he want it, then? Why do *you* think he does?”

"I don't know." Irania smiled. She did have a very charming smile. "I find it suspicious that they're mounting a secret expedition, don't you?"

"It's not much of an expedition."

"No, it's not. More secret than expedition. That's part of what I find so interesting."

We turned our attention to our supper, and a very fine supper it was. Oysters with smoked bacon in chive cream sauce.

Irania said suddenly, "In any case, I do have a partner now, Mr. Bliss."

"Who?"

"That would be telling." She speared a bite of cream-bathed oyster. "But I don't trust him. I would happily exchange him for you. I think you would be more help and less trouble in the end."

"I'm flattered."

She was grinning at me, a very unladylike expression, and I found myself grinning reluctantly back.

"And you're a very pretty young man — especially for such a dry and dusty business. We could have a great deal of fun, you and I."

I was uncomfortably aware I was turning red, but that would have been her aim. "You're a bookseller yourself, Miss Briggs."

"But I'm not a librarian."

"Nor am I. I'm a librivenator."

"You are indeed. And a very fine one, from what I've heard."

She obviously hadn't been talking to anyone from Leslie's Lexicons. "Are you sure your new partner knows his stuff?"

"Oh yes. You needn't worry about me. Though it *is* sweet of you."

She kept up that flirtatious line throughout our meal. I tried, but I didn't seem able to winkle any information from her. The best I could do was make sure she didn't winkle any more from me.

When we had finished our meals right down to the cheese plate, Irania prettily smothered a yawn and announced, "I suppose I should retire. Our boat leaves early tomorrow."

The first ferry out was headed for the island of Barraigh. She must believe that Kiessimul's Castle was one possible destination — which meant she hadn't quite narrowed all the possibilities down. I recalled that, according to Anstruther, Irania Briggs only had half the story.

My gaze fell to my plate. I said quickly, awkwardly, "I'm not leaving on the morning ferry."

"No?"

"No."

There was a note of triumph in her voice as she said, "I'm afraid I am."

I did my best to look as though I were struggling to hide my chagrin. She chuckled. "Sweet dreams, Mr. Bliss."

"And to you, Miss Briggs."

She departed at last, and I could finally relax. I ordered another tankard of ale, which I took up to my room. I glanced over my notes.

For the first time since that morning, I let myself think about Septimus. I wondered how the hunt for the eleventh-century encyclopedia of fairies was going.

I was up early the next morning, carefully noting my dreams in my journal. Writing with a quill pen by candlelight… Well, no secret to what that meant. Freshly polished knives and champagne bottles spilling over — these things took no skill to interpret, even if I hadn't spent most of the night dreaming of having sex with Septimus. Sweet dreams indeed, and totally useless. Why I should be dreaming so intensely and vividly of the man? I hadn't even dreamed of Antony like this when we had still been having our affair.

What I needed to be dreaming was the solution to my mystery, but there was no hint of a breakthrough yet. Still, it was early days.

I was out in front of the inn with my suitcase a short time later, and I made sure that anyone within listening distance heard me order my taxi to the harbor — and to hurry, lest we missed the boat for Barraigh.

Once we were on our way, however, I ordered the taxi to #1 Strathaven Terrace.

The maid opened the door on the second ring. Seeing me, she shook her head. "Dr. Spindrift is still sleeping."

"Still?"

"She's a *goblin*," she said, as though pointing out the obvious — as I suppose she was. "She might sleep for a day or a week or a month."

I was still trying to think what my next move should be as she quietly but firmly shut the door in my face.

* * * * *

The island was in sight, a haze of gold and purple against the bluest sky I had ever seen, when I heard the captain of the *Ròs na Mara* singing.

The words were Gaelic, a language I had scant knowledge of, but the song was still beautiful.

Fath mo mhulaid a bhith ann

'S mi air m'aineoil anns a'ghleann

Fath mo mhulaid a bhith ann

"He is singing a song of exile. It's a song for the Blue Men of the Minch. It is the sad songs they are liking."

I glanced at the speaker, a tall man smoking a pipe. The comfortable scent of the pipe smoke reminded me of Septimus. "What do the words mean?"

"Being here has caused my sorrow. For in the glen, I am a stranger." His smile was wry. "The Blue Men swim out to wreck the ships, but the captain who can speak to them in rhyme and get the last word in — or sing in so sweet a voice — can overcome them."

"I've never heard of the Blue Men. Are they mermen?"

"Sea spirits or ghosts of drowned sailors. They dwell in the underwater caves near here."

"Are you from the island?"

"Aye."

I had my story ready. “I’m a student of architecture come to see the island. If you were me, what on the island would you think it important to see?”

He seemed to give it sincere thought. “There are the old black houses on the beach and the newer white houses, but you will be wanting to see Matheson Castle in Steering Bay. And there are the ruins of the old church at the butte of the island. Och, we’ve many fine buildings, old and new, on the Long Island.”

We fell silent, watching sleek, swift figures streaking through the water toward the ship, but as they drew closer, I saw that they were dolphins racing the ship through the waves and not the legendary Blue Men after all.

The man puffed on his pipe and named a few other places of local interest. He didn’t mention the castle of Agro Urquhart, but neither did I.

Remembering the drawing of Swanhild and the quotation I’d copied down, I pulled out my dream journal and showed the phrase to my fellow passenger.

He smiled faintly. “‘Ge milis a’ mhil, cò dh’imlicheadh o bhàrr dri i.’ Good advice, this is. Honey may be sweet, but no one licks it off a briar.”

I considered this. Safe to say, no friend of Swanhild’s had captioned her portrait.

As we drew closer to the island, we passed the occasional small boat with brown sails raised. I saw what a wild and desolate place we were headed for. There were a few scattered houses, some sheep, and an occasional shaggy-looking cow on a rocky outcropping.

On the maps, the Long Island looked mostly like fish bones or a creature squat and amphibious, but to see it in real life was to be struck by its barren beauty. The endless sweep of sky was cloudless and blue. The smallish hills were covered in golden bracken, purple heather, and blackberries ripening in the sun.

I glanced at the man with the pipe, and he was smiling faintly.

We landed in Steering Bay, the largest town on the entire island — in fact, in the Western Isles. It was a surprise after the initial view of the coastline. Steering Bay was lush with the greenery of trees and gardens. There were many fountains and stone courtyards. Every bit of rock seemed to have been used for decorative purposes, and the purple heather grew between. In the long glass gardens, roses and figs and grapes grew in the August sun.

I was staying at the Imperial Inn in Steering Bay. Despite the grand name, it was a small, unassuming place. I was relieved that there was no sign of Irania Briggs. There were only a few guests, in fact. The proprietress, Mrs. Murdoch, was a busy little woman with a sharp manner barely on the polite side of impatient.

My room had a window that looked over the back garden, but I could smell the sea and hear the gulls.

I asked Mrs. Murdoch if I could use her telefon, and she directed me down the street to a pub. It was a pleasant walk, and no one seemed to be paying me any particular attention. I ordered a pint and made my call to the Museum of the Literary Occult. I was put through to Mr. Anstruther immediately.

"Why have you not rung up before this?" Anstruther demanded as soon as we were connected.

I kept my voice low. "You told me to fone every other night."

He ignored that. "We've had Irania Briggs around here. She told us that she's found another partner and that she is going after the *Faileas a' Chlaidheimh*."

"Who? What's the name of her partner?"

"She didn't say. It's probably a lie."

"Why should she lie about it?"

"Because she is a congenital liar. She lies instantly and instinctively. Why didn't you tell us she had approached you?"

The truth was, I had been so busy preparing for the trip, I hadn't given it much thought. "I suppose I thought you expected her to. That there was no need to confirm it. But she turned up in Oban at the hotel where I was staying. I think she might have followed me to Scotland."

"You're not thinking of pulling something, are you?" Anstruther asked suspiciously.

"What?"

"I wouldn't advise it."

"I wouldn't consider it." I was startled and offended.

Anstruther made a sound of open disbelief. "Young man, you don't know what you're dealing with."

"Maybe you'd better tell me."

"Do the job we've commissioned you to do, and you'll be fine. If you double-cross us —"

I asked indignantly, "You'll what?"

My answer was the sound of a telefon all the way in London being slammed down.

* * * * *

After luncheon I procured a couple of maps and followed Mrs. Murdoch's directions to a local garage that rented automobiles to visitors. The only car available was an old rattletrap of a sportsman's coupe. The garage charged a pretty penny for the privilege, and I was warned of the dangers of driving on the single dirt tracks that served as roadway to most of the island.

The trip from Steering Bay took about forty-five minutes along the paved road to the northernmost tip of the island. I stopped once at the post office in the village of Fivepenny Borve to get further directions to the butte of the island, as all the signs along the deserted road were in Gaelic.

On my drive, I saw the truth of a saying I had once heard about this part of the world: All the sea is islands, and all the islands are lakes.

From the road I could see the stones like cracked teeth in the green graveyard and the crumbled ruins of the old church. I had reached the end of my journey — the end of the island, but there was no castle. I parked and got out and walked to the cliff edge.

No, my eyes were not deceiving me. There was no castle. There had never been a castle here — unless it was witchcraft that had spirited it away.

I got back into the coupe and drove several miles east and discovered that the road to the butte of the island ended in a loop. At the top of this loop was a short walkway to a tiny, rugged island. The island was densely wooded. Thanks to the westerly gales that howled across sea and shore in winter, most of the large island was barren moorland, rock and bog, but the descendants of Agro Urquhart had planted copses of birch and hazel and pine. Somewhere in those woods must be the castle.

It was astonishing how wrong everyone had this — even Dr. Spindrift had said the castle was formerly a church.

When I had stopped earlier in the village to ask directions, I had inquired about the famous sea caves and been told they were dangerous and all but inaccessible by land unless one went through the gardens of the castle — now closed off.

So how did one gain access to the castle?

Apparently one did not.

Even from this distance I could see that there was a tall fence blocking a bridge to the island. The bridge stretched over a very deep chasm. The only way to reach the bridge was by trekking a mile or so through a farmer's pasture.

If my sources had got this wrong, what else had they got wrong? According to the postmistress, the castle was on the other side of the island. I'd assumed she was mistaken or deliberately sending me the opposite way for reasons of her own, but now I wondered.

Climbing back into the coupe, I reversed and tracked my way back to Fivepenny Borve — picking a different place to ask information this time. I had a quick dram at the village pub and questioned the man behind the bar about the little island.

He peered at me disapprovingly over the top of his spectacles. "There's nothing to be seeing there. It's a ruin and not safe."

I thanked him for the information, finished my whisky, and strolled down the sandy road to another shop, this one a tobacconist's. The young woman behind the counter was cheerful and friendly. It occurred to me how few young people I saw on this island. Another sure sign that the old ways were dying out. Not just Old Magick, but all the old ways.

I trotted out my story. I was getting quite glib by then. "I'm a student of architecture. I plan to stay for a couple of weeks and visit some of your black houses. Is there anyone around here who might rent me a room to stay?"

"Aye. There will be Alice Morrison a wee bit down the road. She is running a bed-and-breakfast for the visitors to the island. Not that we are having many visitors this far from Steering Bay."

"You're quite a ways out; that's true. What's the little island with the bridge? I noticed it from the church ruins."

"You will be speaking of Agro's castle." She added, "It is not open to the public. It is not safe at all."

"Pity."

The island and Agro's castle would be accessible at low tide when the sea was out, provided the weather stayed calm. I wasn't worried.

I returned to my car and headed down the sandy road till I came to a sign indicating a bed-and-breakfast in front of a large, white eighteenth-century building.

Alice Morrison turned out to be a tall scarecrow of a woman. She wore mannish trousers, and her accent was tempered by time off the island. She invited me into her parlor and offered me a wee "drappie," which I accepted on the grounds of politeness. A large black cat slept in front of a wide window. A tall bookshelf was full of works on the occult and witchcraft. I felt right at home.

We drank our whisky, and Mrs. Morrison explained that the large old building had once been the village's only school.

"Do you get many visitors out this way?"

"Not many, no. Most of the holidaymakers are not coming out to the islands. There is nothing here for the likes of them."

"There's a lot of history."

"Aye, aye. Sometimes we are getting the history professors from Steering Bay and sometimes from the mainland."

"Anyone lately?"

"No. Not lately. No."

When I finished my whisky, Mrs. Morrison and I came to terms, and then I returned to Steering Bay to get my things.

There was still no sign of Irania Briggs. I packed, paid for my room, and drove back out to Alice Morrison's. She showed me to my room. It was large and airy with old-fashioned wallpaper and a picturesque view of the sea loch.

When I had finished unpacking — which took no time at all — I returned downstairs, and Alice Morrison served tea and bramble muffins. Once again I asked about the sea caves.

According to Alice, the sea caves did not technically belong to anyone, but the only way to access them by land was to go through the wilderness that had once been the grounds of the old castle.

"Is it possible to get in to see the castle?"

She started to speak but then caught herself. "It is possible, but it is not so easy."

"What do you mean?"

"The property is owned by Lord Lovett. Do you know of him?"

I shook my head.

"He is an Englishman with much more money than sense. At one time he was having a grand plan for the castle and the grounds to be made into a museum."

"What happened to that plan?"

Mrs. Morrison said obliquely, "It has fallen through. He did not find a welcome here for his fine plans, Lord Lovett."

"The castle is abandoned now?"

"That is so. Lord Lovett hired Mad Murdo to be acting as his caretaker. But Murdo has moved back to his croft now. I am thinking he will still have the keys."

"Where's this Murdo's croft?"

"After the old churchyard, there is a byroad off the main highway. If you follow the byroad, you will be finding a black house belonging to Mad Murdo. You cannot be missing it."

I wasn't sure about that. I'd missed it the first time. As I turned away, Mrs. Morrison added, "There is a painting of her, you know."

"Of whom?"

"The sea witch."

I didn't know what to say to that.

She smiled. "If you are wanting to see the sea caves, then you must know about the sea witch."

"I've heard of her," I acknowledged.

"The painting hangs in the university museum in Steering Bay. It is supposed to be a great likeness of her, but who would know if that was true?"

We chatted more while I finished my muffins and tea. It was about three in the afternoon when I got back in the coupe and went to find Mad Murdo, the former caretaker of Urquhart's castle.

Now that I knew what I was looking for, it was easier, and I spotted the rough dirt road that diverged from the paved one right away. The first several hundred yards of the lane were very rough and rocky. Although I drove cautiously, I was afraid the old car would be jolted to pieces. I came to a wooden gate, which was not locked, and continued slowly on through a pasture of woolly cattle.

There were two more gates that entailed getting out of the coupe to drag them open, driving through, and then walking back to close them again.

I spotted a leaning water tower and a small, faded sign pointing skyward. It read AGRO'S CASTLE.

The black house was a few yards farther on. It looked derelict, abandoned, but it was not. An old man in a tweed cap came to meet me. A black-and-white collie trotted at his heels. The dog barked, wagging its tail energetically.

I rolled down the window of my auto. "Mr. Murdo?"

"Aye. I am Murdo MacLean."

"My name's Colin Bliss. I'm a student of architecture visiting the island for a week or so. I understand you're the caretaker of Agro's castle. Would it be possible to see it?"

"You are wanting to see the castle?"

"That's right."

"It is a very long time since anyone was coming to see the castle." He eyed me dubiously. "Did you say you are from across the sea, laddie?"

"I am. I'm from Boston. It's a city in the American Confederation." I added, "I want to take some sketches and notes of the buildings and gardens. I'll pay you, of course."

Murdo hesitated. "I will be taking you across, but I will not be staying on with you. It is not a healthy place, Agro's castle."

"What do you mean?"

He said evasively, "The grounds they are being overgrown now; the buildings ruined. I do not think you will be wishing to stay long."

"I'm used to old places. In fact, if you'll loan me the keys, I'll be happy to poke around on my own."

He considered me for what seemed like a long time. He shifted his pipe in his mouth and named a fairly stiff sum.

"All right, but as we're getting such a late start, I might wish to come back another day or two. The fee will have to cover that."

"You will not be wishing to come back." Mad Murdo sounded confident.

He went back to the house, and I got out of the car. The sun was surprisingly strong, though the breeze from the sea had a salty bite to it.

Mad Murdo reappeared with wire hoop of keys, some modern and some very old, elaborate, and beautiful ones, in various conditions of rust and tarnish.

"How long will it take to walk?"

He looked at me, looked at my shoes, and said, "Fifteen minutes, I am thinking. If you are not falling into the sea.

It was a little more than fifteen minutes, even though I was not falling into the sea. I did think I might be gored by an overly interested long-horned bull before we reached the walkway. Mad Murdo's collie chased off the shaggy beast, to my relief and my tour guide's amusement.

We reached the bridge, which looked relatively modern in construction. It bounced gently beneath the pound of our footfalls as we crossed. Below us, the green-blue tide swirled around dark rocks netted in golden seaweed. Seals dotted the water, making for the white sand of the beach at the foot of the cliff.

At last we came to the other side and a view of flat open fields in dazzlingly bright sunshine. The sea sparkled around us, and ahead lay the dark green woods. Everywhere was the feel of great age and timelessness.

Mad Murdo gestured to the left, and we crossed the clearing, where a couple of incurious sheep grazed. From there we took a small path through the woods, and came in good time to the castle.

"The castle of Agro Urquhart," Murdo announced.

As castles went, it was not much larger than the average-sized mansion. I had expected the usual moss-covered tumble of broken stone like the old church on the butte, but this looked like a small version of the follies and castles one saw in the mainland cities. It was clear the castle had been midrenovation when the Englishman's money — or interest — had run out.

My guide looked at me and laughed.

"I thought it would be a ruin," I admitted.

"It is that. You just cannot be seeing from this distance."

The dog darted forward, snuffling through the undergrowth. We followed more slowly.

We found ourselves before the tall spiked gates — something I associated with European Alliance castles rather than Scottish.

As though reading my mind, Murdo said, "Lord Lovett built the fence. He was not knowing then that the problem would not be in keeping people out, but in getting people to come."

The posts of the gate were lashed together with rusty chain. Murdo unlocked a small side gate that opened with a protest of corroded hinges. The dog wriggled through, and Murdo and I followed it into the strangled garden. All around us was the moist fragrance of age and mold and heat.

Green creepers tumbled down in cascades of vines. Tall green shapes — moss-covered statues — rose spectral-like from the verdant waves. Here and there a hand stuck out in supplication or a head peeped up from the greenery. We picked our way through a path nearly closed off by rioting undergrowth, until we came to steps leading to a terrace paved in some kind of quartz. Beneath the dust and dead leaves, an occasional sparkle caught the shifting sunlight. Tufts of grass grew in the cracks.

Tall double doors stood before us, a crest featuring what appeared to be fanged boars chiseled into the peeling surface.

The dog, which had been rooting through the crust of leaves and debris, froze and stared off toward the garden, hackles raised.

"What does he see?" I knew the question was foolish. How should Murdo know what the dog sensed?

Murdo did not answer. Did not even look at the dog. He unlocked the door and handed over the jangling hoop of keys.

"You're leaving, then?" I was surprised but mostly pleased. I wanted the freedom to hunt without anyone observing me.

Murdo nodded, avoiding my eyes. Clearly he was in a hurry to leave this haunted place, and I couldn't entirely blame him. The dog approached the edge of the terrace, huff still raised, ears back.

"If you will be leaving the keys at the croft when you are done, Mr. Bliss?" Murdo didn't wait for my reply. He whistled to the dog, which abandoned its aggressive stance and trotted after him.

I watched them hurry away, man and dog, scuttling along the broken walkway and then disappearing in the maze of green. The side gate clanged behind them like a muted bell.

CHAPTER NINE

Pushing open the heavy doors, I was surprised to see bright sunshine illuminating the great rectangular entrance hall before me. The floor was a blue and yellow checkerboard. A wide staircase of marble and ornate metal wound up before splitting into a Y. At its base was a pile of debris where workmen had started renovation and then abandoned it. One old screwdriver lay on a workbench in front of a yellow marble fireplace.

It was surprisingly chilly, given the warmth of the day. It was not the chill of the supernatural, though. At least I didn't think so, although that was not my area of expertise.

I fastened the hoop of keys to my belt and started up the stately staircase. Midway, I was level with the gigantic windows at the back of the hall. Through the dirty glass, I could see the sparkling blue breadth of the ocean.

At the Y, I continued to the right to the first level. At the top of the stairs was a cache of signs for ticket window and fees and whatnot. Marble columns lined the long, stark hallway, but all other character had been stripped away or repainted. My footsteps had a dead and dusty echo as I walked down the hall looking for the library.

I found it, a great empty shell of a room. The furniture had been removed. The shelving had been repainted white, but of course, all the books were long gone.

It didn't matter. This was all too modern to be of any use. I might not truly be an expert on architecture, but even I knew that I was looking at a much-renovated and gutted shell of the original structure. Agro's original castle could not have looked anything like this.

Walking from barren room to barren room, I was more cognizant than ever of what an impossible task lay before me.

It took well over an hour, but when I had satisfied myself that there was nothing left inside the castle that could be of possible use, I went downstairs, locked the door behind me, and stepped out onto the terrace.

The warmth of the sunshine and the scent of the ocean and vegetation came as a relief after the stale paint and wood dust of the interior.

I decided that I might as well have a look for the chapel mentioned in the Burnham book — the chapel where Swanhild was reputed to be buried.

Moving to the terrace balustrade, I scanned the jungle of undergrowth and spotted something like a small dome overgrown with vines. My leap of excitement faded almost at once. Whatever that structure was, it wasn't a chapel. It was too small, for one thing, and for another, it was planted squarely in what would have been the front yard of the castle.

I jumped over the balustrade and landed in the shoulder-high grass. I approached the dome, the hoop of keys jangling on my belt.

From a few feet away, it appeared to be gray stone within cobwebs of vines. It was not the right shape to be an obelisk, this architectural oddity, and as I drew nearer, I saw that it was made of weathered marble and carved with runes and strange markings.

The structure looked older than the castle — or at least the latest renovation of the castle. If only I were the student of architecture I pretended to be, I'd know what it was I was looking at.

Was it an entrance of some kind? But an entrance to what? There was no building beyond this archway. Perhaps another structure had once stood behind this one?

The screen of vines hung like a veil in the hot, suddenly windless air. Peering closer, I tried to decipher the characters carved into the two columns. The letters, if letters they were, were unfamiliar to me. The other markings looked like pictographs. Ships and stars and lightning bolts...and one symbol repeated over and over: that of a crested snake.

There weren't a lot of snakes in Scotland. Grass snakes, slow worms, and adders. Nothing crested. I wiped my forehead, pushing back my hair. Sweat trickled between my shoulder blades, prickled my scalp.

I circled the archway, tearing vines free, looking at the strange markings of long-ago battles. I didn't have to be a historian to make sense of boats and battles. The fire and sword symbols surely had to do with warfare against the Sodreys Sea Raiders. But that peculiar coiling snake... Was it some reference to Christianity? The serpent in the Garden of Eden?

Donnie Large had been one of the most powerful Christian kings, and according to what I'd read, Agro Urquhart had attempted to bring the sect of Christianity to the Western Isles.

I peered more closely. Every inch of the archway appeared to be carved with these scripts and runes and pictures. Of course, they might be merely decorative. The structure itself might be merely decorative. A garden feature of some kind? I moved back to scrutinize it.

Two pedestals and an arch about seven feet tall in height. An ominous crack — like a lightning bolt — lanced through the lintel.

Interesting, but probably not important. It was surely more pressing that I find the chapel. That at least would confirm Swanhild's fate — and give me a starting point for my hunt.

I turned to walk back to the castle and the vantage point offered by the terrace, but as I climbed back through the fallen tree limbs and broken statuary, I puzzled over the idea of an archway leading nowhere.

Not very likely, was it?

I turned back, wading once more through the grass and brambles. Kneeling at the base of the pedestal, I began to tear away the grass and weeds and vines. The roots had knotted into the soil, creating a tough mat. I needed something to dig with. Some kind of tool.

I jogged back to the castle, let myself in the heavy front doors, and snatched up the screwdriver on the workbench. I returned to the base of the arch and started jabbing into the mat of dirt and roots.

My heart skipped as I heard the unmistakable sound of metal on wood. There *was* something beneath the archway.

Feverishly I scraped and clawed at the mat of weeds and at last uncovered the octagonal outline of what appeared to be a wooden lid in the ground.

I sat back on my haunches, trying to consider what this might be. It measured about three feet by three feet. Was it a well? A cistern? Could it be a doorway? A door to a storm cellar or an underground tunnel?

I could see the lid or door had a handle — a metal loop, heavily rusted. And beneath the metal loop was the flared outline of a keyhole.

Pawing through the ring of keys, I examined each one. There were about fifty or so, old and new. I was looking for something old and — judging by the size of the keyhole — large. I found it by the design on its bow: a boar's head.

The key's wards were large and uncomplicated. A very old key indeed, and yet it appeared to be steel.

I worked the key into the hole. The lock was stiff, and I expected anything — the key not to fit, the lock to be broken — but as the key was steel, perhaps so were the internal workings of the lock, and thus it had a better chance of withstanding time and weather and usage.

With a bit of effort, the key slipped into the lock, and I began to turn it. And then it stopped dead. Jammed.

I applied pressure, but it would not budge. I took it out, wiped it, tried again. I wriggled it. Nothing. I removed the key and considered.

As badly as I now wanted that door open, how was I supposed to explain it if I broke the lock or one of the keys?

All at once I had the uncanny sense of being watched. I rose, looking uneasily around the overgrown jungle. Late-afternoon sun flooded down the vegetation, glinting and flashing in the windless sunlight. A sea of green lay motionless in the heat. A drowsy silence pervaded the grounds — and the feeling of not being alone persisted.

I wiped my forehead. “Hello?” I called.

I did not expect an answer. Would have jumped a foot if I’d received one. And yet the silence put me on edge.

My need to get the door open overrode my concern for the lock. I fished the screwdriver out of the grass and pried at the lock. I poked and prodded, felt something give. I slipped the key back in. This time the lock seemed to budge forward a centimeter.

Applying slow, even pressure, I twisted the key in the tumbler. This was nothing like the modern locks installed on the double doors of the castle itself.

At last the steel shaft made its full turn. Triumphantly I cleared the remaining dirt and debris out of the way, tearing out the last clumps of weeds and vines blocking the door’s outward sweep. I pried at the rusted loop of door handle, and it lifted away enough for me to slip my hand beneath. I tugged.

The angle was awkward, and the door was nearly as heavy as stone. I pulled and panted and wondered if I would put my back out, but grudgingly, reluctantly, the round door pulled away a few grimy inches, dirt and pebbles falling inside and rattling eerily into the emptiness below.

I gazed down into a black hole — and a narrow flight of stairs vanishing into that inkwell.

Dropping to my haunches once more, raking my hair out of my eyes, I gazed downward. A cold breath of chilly air, as from a cellar, wafted upward. It had a dead quality. How long ago had this door been shut? A century? Was I breathing centuries-old air?

I inched cautiously back, stretched out on the grass, and peered over the edge. I couldn't see anything beyond the short flight of stairs. It was impenetrable darkness.

There was a torch in the glove box of the coupe, but that was parked back at Mad Murdo's croft. No quick and easy walk back there. I looked up at the sky. The sun was starting to fade, the day softening. Sunset was not until around eight, but it had been a long day, and I was tired, and — I might as well be honest — the idea of poking around here as the shadows lengthened was not appealing.

Perhaps Septimus's warnings had impressed me more than I thought.

Better to get a fresh start in the morning. Sunrise was around four thirty. Tomorrow would offer a good long day to work undisturbed.

Having settled on a plan, I shoved the door back into place and relocked it. I covered it up with loose vines and leaves and grass. At last I rose, brushing off my hands. Returned to the castle, I locked and tested the tall double doors. I headed back down the path to the entrance gates, walking in and out of shadows and sunlight, passing the occasional burst of flowering vine.

Reaching the gates — annoyed to feel relieved to do so — I pushed through them. I locked them carefully behind me, although I couldn't imagine there was much danger of anyone trespassing.

It was colder crossing the bridge on the way back to the main island; the tide was high now, and the mist seemed to rise and sparkle in the afternoon air. An unearthly moaning seemed to drift up from the water below. I shivered and walked faster.

The shaggy Highland cattle paid no attention to me on my return journey through the scrubby green pasture.

As I drew near Mad Murdo's black house, I considered whether it made sense to hang on to the keys for a few days. I could ask to borrow them again, but that was undoubtedly going to draw attention to my activities. If I kept them, I could come and go as I pleased. I fully intended to explore the tunnel, and I might need to get back into the castle. And what about the chapel?

I stopped walking and began to sort through the keys. The castle key, the key to the tunnel — those I already knew. I sifted quickly through the others. There was a long key with a cross at the end of its bow. This would surely be the key to the chapel — assuming it still existed. With a guilty glance at Murdo's cottage, I slipped it off the ring with the other two I wanted, and dropped them into my pocket.

When I reached the black house, Murdo was having what appeared to be his evening meal. He took the ring of keys without a glance and hung them on the wall hook.

I bade him good night and left, hiking back to where I had parked my automobile. Dew beaded the windshield. Twilight was approaching quickly.

* * * * *

"And wasn't I just saying that it would be yourself coming any moment," Mrs. Morrison said as I stepped inside the kitchen door.

She was mashing potatoes and turnips together in a big pan, but though the comment was addressed to me, she was smiling at the kitchen's other inhabitant.

I came to a dead stop.

Septimus Marx stood in the opposite doorway. Mrs. Morrison's large black cat was cradled in his arms. From where I stood, I could practically hear the cat purring as Septimus stroked its shiny black fur.

"What are you doing here?" I asked. My voice was harsh — maybe because I was unsettled by my delight at the unexpected sight of him.

The V of Septimus's eyebrows rose. "The same as you, I imagine, Mr. Bliss."

"Was it after being a good day for you?" Mrs. Morrison inquired.

I recovered enough to say, "Yes. It was."

"Was Murd —"

"Yes," I cut her off quickly. "Very helpful."

"We will be having our supper in five minutes or so."

"I'll need to freshen up." I had to pass Septimus. He moved aside, his attention apparently all on the cat.

I expected him to follow me, but he didn't, so I was able to relax a bit as I washed up, changed my shirt, and came back down. I could hear Septimus talking to Mrs. Morrison. His voice was too low to make out the words, but I heard her response.

"Not so many visitors these days, no. And those that come are not coming for the same reasons as they once did. It is nice to be having guests again."

I reentered the kitchen as the cat scrabbled out of Septimus's arms. He let it go and, after an unfathomable look at me, went upstairs to wash.

I said to Mrs. Morrison, "I didn't know Mr. Marx was staying here."

"Nor did I. Mr. Marx only arrived this afternoon." She put me to work straightaway setting the table.

* * * * *

The meal consisted of leek soup and something called mince and tatties, which turned out to be beef chopped up in the turnip and potato mash. It was simple but tasty food, and there was plenty of it. Septimus ate heartily in between chatting with Mrs. Morrison about the island's history. I noticed he confined his questions to the nonarcane.

I learned a great deal about fishing and weaving and cutting peat that night.

When the meal was over, Mrs. Morrison prepared something called Gaelic coffee, a concoction of coffee, cream, sugar, and single malt scotch whisky. Septimus asked if he might smoke his pipe, and our hostess gave him permission, adding that the late Mr. Morrison had smoked a pipe, and she missed the smell of it.

Finally, after getting out a chessboard and pieces for us, Mrs. Morrison took herself off to bed.

"Did you want a game?"

I shrugged.

Septimus set up the game board while we listened to the rumble of the old plumbing.

When the pipes overhead had fallen silent, I asked, "The truth. Why are you here?"

He placed the final carved piece on the board. "You know why I'm here." He met my eyes, and his own were greener than the machair pastures near the ocean.

I smiled a little bitterly. "You missed me?"

"It's not inconceivable. You're a charming bedmate. But we both know why I've followed you. I'm chagrined it took me so long to realize the book you're hunting."

I said nothing, waiting.

"*Faileas a' Chlaidheimh.*" Septimus pronounced it with the lilt of the islanders. The candles in the room flared and then went low, almost guttering before they resumed normal proportions.

"It doesn't exist, according to the imperial archives."

"And yet that is the book you seek."

I lowered my voice. "All right. What if it is? Wouldn't you want it found if it does exist?"

"No."

I stared at him.

"No," Septimus repeated. "That is a book that would be better lost to time."

"How can you say that?" I truly couldn't understand his logic. Our entire branch of the service was dedicated to retrieving and preserving these literary works. It was the sole reason for our existence.

"Most certainly the grimoire cannot fall into the hands of Aengus Anstruther."

"Better preserved in the Museum of the Literary Occult than destroyed."

He sighed, and the weariness of that sigh — like a parent struggling for patience with a child — sent my own temper flaring like the candles a moment before.

I jumped to my feet. "I don't agree that there are books too dangerous to exist. It's against everything we believe in the Societas Magicke. It defies reason."

"I don't expect you to agree or understand, but you will obey in this." Septimus rose also. We glared at each other across the table.

"Obey?"

"Obey," he repeated flatly.

I laughed. It wasn't much of a laugh, but Septimus's face darkened. "Don't push your luck, Colin. If you give it up now, leave the island, and go spend your holiday fishing or hiking, no one will ever know what you were contemplating."

"Is that supposed to be a generous offer?"

"It's more than generous, as you'd realize if you weren't so pigheaded."

"I'm not ashamed of what I'm contemplating."

"You should be."

"The devil I should. You have no right to order me away. I'm acting as a free agent in this."

"You're not a free agent," he snapped. "You're an officer of the Arcane Services. You're a librivenator, in the name of All! You can't blithely decide to use your skills and training for your own gain."

"It's not my gain. I told you —"

"I know what you told me. You plan to use your experience for another book or for a series of articles. That may be the way things work in the colonies, but it doesn't work that way here."

Of course the more Septimus talked to me — talked *down* to me — in that arrogant, high-handed manner, the more angry and stubborn I grew. If I were honest, no small portion of my anger was the confirmation that he had seduced me for his own ends, to distract me from my quest apparently. And that I'd let him.

Even now I was painfully, intensely aware of him as he stood a few feet from me.

"I'm already conscious that I don't meet the expectations of the London branch. Well, what do you want? I'm just a simple native son from across the Great Big Sea. We're more straightforward in our dealings. It's our job to hunt books, and that's what we do. And where I come from, book destroyers are considered the lowest of low."

Septimus went white with anger. His eyes looked black — for one moment I was almost frightened of him.

He said with what seemed to be an almost painful control, "You have no idea what you're talking about."

"I know I have small chance of finding *The Sword's Shadow* —" I paused at the way he tensed when I spoke name of the grimoire aloud — "but if the book exists, it should be preserved, and if that means handing it over to a private collection —"

He crossed the room. His fingers bit into the muscles of my arms. "You're a fool if you think I'll allow it."

"Really? What will you do? Kill me?" I added bitterly, "Fuck me?"

To my astonishment, Septimus's mouth came down on my own, hot and hungry.

When he raised his head, his eyes looked strange, almost desperate, and blood thumped in my ears — and my cock — in response to that silent gaze.

His head lowered again, this time in a kiss of deliberate and coaxing sweetness.

Belatedly I remembered the train to Oban and the same expert seduction.

I bunched my fists in his shirt and shoved him back. He staggered slightly.

I said — more breathlessly than I'd have liked — "I think we've reached a philosophical impasse, Magister."

I'm not sure he even heard me. Septimus stepped toward me, his hands covered mine, and he drew me forward — and to my confusion, I let that tide pull me along, my arms slipping around his neck as though I had lost all will of my own.

He was doing it again. He was using sex to distract me — and I was going along with it. *Why* was I going along with it? If only I could believe he was using some kind of magick on me, but I was pretty sure that was not the case as his feverish mouth found the hollow at the base of my throat where the pulse was hammering in a dead giveaway.

"This doesn't change anything…"

"No. It doesn't," he whispered.

I shivered, already lost, as his hands dug into my buttocks, fitting us together.

What followed was urgent — near-frenzied — and for those too-few minutes, all-consuming. Hands shaking, we undid buckles, buttons, and zippers, freeing ourselves from the confines of clothing as we fell on Mrs. Morrison's love seat, sending the cat leaping to safety.

"What is this effect you have on me?" Septimus groaned. His hand locked in my hair as though he wanted to shake me.

I kissed him and kept kissing him. Maybe it was the sheer need to convince myself it was really happening, or maybe it was the taste of him, but I couldn't seem to stop. Even the fleeting idea of our landlady coming downstairs to check out untoward noises didn't cool my ardor.

From the love seat, we slid to the carpet, Septimus on his back, his cock jutting up from the silky nest at his groin, and me thrusting fiercely on top. Our straining cocks stroked against each other, fencing, rigid, dry, and smooth, but soon enough slick with the first drops of semen.

I thought I would go mad with the sheer alarming pleasure of it. I buried my face in Septimus's throat, inhaling that mixture of scents peculiar to him — pipe tobacco, violet leaf, black pepper… I moaned his name.

The next instant, all my anger and energy were releasing in long, powerful surges.

Septimus rolled me onto my back, his weight pinning me to the floorboards, his cock jabbing me hard as he thrust.

"*Colin,*" he grated. The rush of release splashed between the press of our bodies.

Afterward we lay unmoving, listening to the floorboards settle and the wind howling outside.

CHAPTER TEN

I was up and out of the house at first light the next morning. Up before our hostess. Up even before the chickens. The old house was a dark and silent oblong against the gray sky as I drove away.

Parked over the small swell of hill, I pulled the electric torch from the glove box, double-checked I had the keys. The wind was whistling a mournful tune as I walked across Mad Murdo's pasture. It reminded me uncomfortably of the night before, of those long, strange minutes while Septimus and I had lain on Mrs. Morrison's hard wood floor and tried to catch our breath. We had said nothing to each other. Even now I couldn't think of what there was to say.

The pasture smelled of sweet grass and manure. The cows were motionless dark figures in the gloom — still sleeping, I supposed. Reaching the final gate, I climbed over and started across the bridge to the island. The sea formed a silver path to the edge of the world.

The sun was just coming up as I crossed the clearing and entered the woods. I had wondered if I would have trouble finding the path back, but I didn't. As I came out of the woods and spied the castle, I heard the sudden sweet song of a thrush.

I took it to be a good omen. Each time I had heard the thrush before, I had experienced some instance of Old Magick. Perhaps this was confirmation that I was on the right track.

Or perhaps it simply meant that thrushes lived in these woods. They were plentiful along the coast of Scotland. It was only too easy to find omens once you started looking for them.

I unlocked the gate and went through, retracing my steps to the strange structure in the garden. Thrush's song or no, I was uneasy. I put it down to Septimus and his cryptic warnings of the night before.

Still, there were the branches and withering vines with which I had concealed the octagonal entrance in the ground — and the screwdriver lay where I had left it at the base of one of the pillars.

The lock was stiff, but it opened with less effort than I'd had to use the day before. I dragged the door up and stared down into that pool of black nothingness, with only a pale glimmer of stairs to reassure that there was anything beyond.

I started down the stairs. It was a short flight, and about ten feet down it branched off into a tunnel — really more of a stone walkway about five feet high. I had to stoop, hunched over as I traveled to the end, which opened to a room. My torch illuminated a small, octagon-shaped, windowless chamber just tall enough for me to stand upright, my hair brushing the stone ceiling. It was dry and permeated with the familiar peppery smell of old paper and books.

The torch beam played over the shelves lining each wall. Sparkling white dust lay like a blanket over everything — shed from the stone interior itself. The shelves were crowded with books.

For a second I thought that my quest would end here, and it was so relatively easy that I was stunned. But as I began to walk the room, my torch playing over the crowded shelves, I realized that the volumes crowded there seemed to be ledgers — household accountings — rather than books.

There was a carved wooden box in the middle of the nearest shelf.

I propped the torch and lifted the lid of the box. Inside were rolls of yellowed papers and faded ink. Warrants and deeds and patents. Family papers.

It appeared that I had stumbled upon some kind of steward's room. A muniment room: a chamber in a castle or a church where important historical documents and records were stored.

This was a find of historical significance — possibly worth a small fortune in its own right — but it did not appear to be what I was searching for.

I felt an odd sense of relief — which was immediately replaced by impatience. I was letting Septimus's conservative and destructive attitude influence my own.

Running the flashlight beam like a finger of light across the spines of the ledgers, I recognized that these long-dead stewards of the Urquharts' had sensibly laid everything out by year: 1845, 1739, 1616…

I don't know how long I spent checking the contents of the shelves — certainly an hour or two went by in my searching for any volume that appeared out of place. I sensed no hint of magus. Certainly nothing *looked* remotely like a grimoire or spell book.

Tracking back to the oldest of the ledgers, I lifted it carefully from the shelf and was pleased — and surprised — to find that it held together firmly. The stone vault was proof against light and moisture as well as insects and vermin. I rested the flashlight on the shelf and opened the ledger — then stopped in shock at the unmistakable sound of someone in the passageway behind me.

I grabbed the torch and spun around.

Daylight pooled at the far end of the stone tunnel, and the stairs leading up to the world above were empty.

No one — nothing — stood in the passageway.

Nothing now anyway.

I tried to recall the sound. I had been sure it was the scrape of a shoe sole on stone, but perhaps it had been a leaf scratching along the granite. Perhaps a squirrel had scampered down and then darted up and away.

Perhaps — or perhaps not.

It would be the simplest thing in the world to just...close the door and fasten the lock once more. If someone shut me in that muniment room, it would all be over. The chamber was airtight; one way in and one way out — and once the batteries of my torch failed, as pitch-black as the tomb. No one would find me. No one would know where to look. No one would hear my screams. I would die there.

These thoughts raced feverishly through my brain as I ducked out of the chamber and sprinted for the opening. As I tore back up the stairs, my heart thundering in my ears, Septimus's warning seemed to ring in my ears.

The entrance to the tunnel was unobstructed, and I burst up into sunlight and fresh air.

All was silent and green and bright. I knelt in the grass, breathing hard. That was alarm, not exertion. I had dismissed Septimus's warnings — threats — whatever they were, but it occurred to me that there was more than one kind of danger in this hunt.

Nothing moved, not even a branch stirred.

Yet I was sure I had heard something…

Again I tried to identify the sound in my memory. I was sure it was not my imagination. It had to have been some animal in the undergrowth. That would certainly be expected. I stared at the soft ground around the entrance. There were footprints, but they appeared to be mine.

I realized I was still clutching one of the ledgers. As I was in no hurry to go back into that paper-lined tomb, I sat down on the ground, back against one of the columns of the archway, and examined the heavy book.

I scrutinized the parchment binding, the date inked in copperplate on the spine: *1616*.

Carefully I opened it, cautious of the browned edges of the paper. The book was in mint condition, pages ruled and columned and full of dates and figures in a neat hand. It seemed a record of stable accounts: hay and corn, riding horses shod, carriage horses shod…

I closed my eyes and perused it.

Cold hands, pinched mouth, specks of snuff…spilled whisky…a stumbling walk with someone…someone unseen…along the cliff. A sharp blow between the shoulder blades and a dizzying whirling impression of water, rocks…and nothing.

I opened my eyes, feeling queasy.

That had never happened before. I'd never perused a book or a ledger written by someone who had been murdered. Or if I had, I hadn't perused that particular and final moment.

I swallowed hard.

Murder.

Well, unpleasant secrets were sometimes discovered in a perusing, but that was certainly the most unpleasant I'd yet come across.

This was a violent place indeed.

I closed the ledger. A historian would have had a field day with this treasure trove, but remembering how little time I had for my endeavor, I needed to return to the hunt. Remembering that I had left my flashlight down below, I went back down the stairs — with many uneasy looks over my shoulder — replaced the ledger, and resurfaced again, torch in hand.

I slid the heavy door back into place and locked it once more. Once again I had that uncomfortable sensation of being watched. I looked around, but there was nothing out of the ordinary.

Now what?

To be absolutely positive the grimoire was not somehow concealed below — perhaps bound in the boards of a household-account book — I would have to go back and search more carefully through the volumes stored there, but I had sensed nothing veneficus, nothing of the magus. My instinct told me the grimoire was not there.

In any case, I was too uneasy to stay belowground examining ledgers now. For the time being I would leave the muniment room locked and focus on trying to find another possible hiding place for the grimoire — assuming it had ever made it to Agro's castle and Swanhild's keeping.

Why did I keep thinking it had?

Librivenator instinct or lack of imagination? I wasn't sure.

I walked back to the castle and mounted the terrace, which offered the best vantage point without going back inside. From there I tried to trace the snarl of paths that vanished into the jungle. I came reluctantly to the conclusion that there was no way around it; I'd simply have to follow one after another until I had combed the entire grounds.

I was looking for a tower, separate towers having been one of the most popular places for the practice of magick during the twelfth through fifteenth centuries. I spent the next few sweaty hours climbing up staircases that led nowhere or through the debris of the ruined garden.

I found the ruins of the tower near the sandy shore.

Sitting on the broken wall, I gazed out to sea, shading my eyes from the glitter of the sun on the water. This was probably the end of the hunt. The shattered tower spoke of enchantment gone wrong.

What else could explain this rubble? There were no marks of fire or sword, and Scotland did not suffer tidal waves, but something had knocked this tower clean in half. Sent the top half sailing yards back to the grassy shelf. Knocked the lower half to bits.

However, I had read not a single story about this tower and its destruction.

After a time I rose and began to prowl the water's edge, looking for the sea caves. If they had been used as a prison, they must be reasonably accessible and fairly close to the main structure of the castle. Yet I could not find them.

The island seemed to offer more mysteries than it solved.

Still, I had nearly a week and a half left of my holiday; there was nothing to be lost by continuing to explore. In fact, I had nothing else to do, and no one to spend this time with. Unless Septimus…

Impatiently I put that thought away. Surely I was not so stupid as to start thinking Septimus's attentions were anything but an attempt to distract me from my quest.

I found the chapel late that afternoon. A short overgrown track led through what had once been an elegant avenue of trees. Memorial statues, characteristic of the maudlin nineteenth century, flanked the small square chapel on each side. The building was made of stone. It had a high, peaked roof and arched doors.

I studied it for a time. I'd been expecting a structure from the fourteenth century. I might not be a true expert in architecture, but even I could recognize that this was of a much-later date. *Was* this the resting place of Swanhild Somerhairle? Could there be yet another chapel somewhere in this seaside jungle?

Perhaps the Burnham book had been wrong; most of my other sources were. What if the reference to "chapel" was actually the old ruined kirk back on the large island?

I walked around the small building and returned to the front. As I looked more closely at the rough-hewn foundation, I determined that it was, in fact, a very old building but, like the castle itself, had been remodeled in the mid-eighteenth century with oval windows and ornate stonework. Utterly out of place on this windswept island.

The two doors contained in a double arch were black with age. They looked solid and immovable.

I checked the keys I had transferred to my own key ring and found the one I was looking for, the old one with the small cross on the bow. I inserted it into the lock. It turned stickily. I pushed hard, harder, put my shoulder to it — and the door flew open.

I stumbled into a stone vestibule. This was about six feet square and led to another set of double doors. These were beautiful, ornately carved doors of something that looked very like ivory. There was no handle or keyhole. I gave the doors a push, and they swung open, creaking, scraping against the stone floor.

Even as my eyes adjusted to the dim light, I was aware that something was wrong.

The inside of the chapel was absolutely bare of any adornment. No stained glass or carvings, no painted beams. No cross.

No cross.

Beyond strange. The islands were almost entirely given over to Christianity. Here was one of the greatest bastions of the sect, yet in this chapel it had been seemingly repudiated. The original intent had not been so spartan, because I could see the faded marks of where a cross had once hung and the overlay of black wash over formerly painted beams and pews. At some point, some unknown Urquhart chieftain had stripped the chapel bare of any decoration.

Nor was the desecration recent. This had happened decades — perhaps hundreds of years — ago. The interior of the chapel was absolutely and utterly bare. Yet the building itself had not been razed to the ground. What did it signify?

I walked down the aisle, past plain wooden pews furred in dust. Where the altar would have once stood was an empty square. Two stone tombs stood at either the end of the square. Not lying flat, but standing upright. Diminutive effigies of a man and woman made of bronze, not marble, and chiseled in perfect detail. The man held an upraised sword and a round targe. I recognized him at once, which I suppose indicated how very good the portraits were that I'd seen.

A plaque at his feet bore the legend:

Agro Urquhart

1352 - 1403

Lord of the Western Isles

There was a Gaelic — not Latin — inscription on the plaque.

Chan 'eil sinne air ar slighe a chall. Tha ar slighe air sinne a chall.

I took out my notepad and wrote it down. On the other side of the square stood the likeness of a shy and mousy-looking woman. I had only seen a sketch of Swanhild, but clearly this was not she. It would not be Agro's first wife. The betrayer? The witch? Urquhart's chieftain would hardly choose to face eternity with her at his side. No, this would be her successor, the woman he had married within a year of his marriage to Swanhild.

No warrior maid, this. So who was she? A bride from the mainland, one of the books had said.

There were other statues lining the walls of the chapel — a ghostly company standing in the shadows — but judging by their dress, these were all more recent family members.

So the family crypt must be here somewhere.

I looked around, looked down, and realized I must be standing on the entrance: a broad marble slab in front of the vanished altar. It could be pried up and mortared down as needed.

I didn't have the tools for prying marble slabs, even if I knew with certainty what I sought was beneath this floor. And was there any point to that? Would they hide the *Faileas a' Chlaidheimh* in the family crypt?

They? They who?

This was the problem. I didn't know enough of the circumstances of the grimoire's disappearance to guess with any accuracy.

This did raise the question of whether Urquhart would have buried Swanhild in the family crypt. According to Burnham, she had been laid to rest in the chapel, but given the sinister absence of information on her death, I wondered about the veracity of that.

What would have been done with her? Could there be another tomb? Another resting place?

Did I need to do more exploring of the jungle outside? I really hadn't much enthusiasm left for it.

I walked the long side of the chapel, across, then down the other side, where the aisle continued on back past where the altar had stood. This brought me to an arched opening set midway in the rear stone wall.

There appeared to be some kind of extra enclosure or extension barred by an elaborate iron grille in a design of vines — no, seaweed — with traces of gilt yet remaining.

In the center of the gate was a large septegram, or seven-point star, a sacred symbol to the fey.

This was truly irregular. Why had every religious symbol been eradicated from the chapel but this — the only one that could not have been original to the design?

I stared through the grille into the shadows beyond. A few stone steps led out of sight. A sliver of light showed from some unseen source.

An uneasy mixture of excitement and foreboding slithered down my spine. I wanted to see whatever lay behind this gate — and I was very much doubting the wisdom of taking one step farther.

There was no handle to the gate. No lock. No keyhole. Nothing. No hinges to indicate it was intended ever to open. Perhaps it was not a gate. Perhaps it was a barrier to whatever lay beyond.

Or perhaps it had a hidden lock.

I studied the long, sharp points of the star. This star was the only real possibility for a lock or a handle.

I felt over the rough and rusty metal, tried twisting and turning the arms of the star, and felt a certain play in its design. I gave it a tug, and the entire star turned with a rusty *squawk* like the wheel on a ship. At the same time I felt a metallic stirring somewhere in the gate, a vibration similar to harp strings.

Minutes later, with some scrapes on my hands, I had the gate inching sideways, and as it moved, I could hear the invisible bolts of a secret mechanism unaffected by time or rust, the masterpiece of some long-ago ironworker.

To my right, I could see a hairline of space running down the stone frame of the gate, top to bottom. Did the gate slide inside the wall? I pushed it, but nothing happened. I pulled, and the gate swung toward me heavily, with a mewing cry from ancient, well-concealed hinges.

The archway stood open, framing a section of blackened stone wall and bare stone floor.

The rubble of dust and scattered stone shed by the beamed plaster overhead crunched underfoot as I advanced through the doorway and started down the stairs.

This chamber seemed much older than the rest of the chapel, and it was in bad repair. The only source of watery daylight was a small round window opaque with dust, very high up in the wall of the stairwell. The silence had a chill quality to it.

Other than the risk of falling in the gloom, there was nothing particularly alarming about this — yet I had the strong feeling that I was trespassing where I was unwelcome and unwanted.

The staircase wound down to another archway, which looked into a small narrow chamber. Most of the chamber was taken up by a black marble tomb. The hair on the back of my neck rose.

On the lid of the tomb was a bronze likeness of a woman reclining on a bed of seaweed. With one hand, she held a large conch seashell to her ear. Her head was turned toward the archway and gave the illusion that she had been listening to the music of the sea when her attention had been caught by my intrusion. Even in the bronze work, I recognized the wide eyes and the haughty curve of her mouth.

Swanhild Somerhairle.

It was true, then. After her death she had been buried in the chapel. But how had she died? If she was truly an adulterous wife, would she have been buried here? Even more strange were the symbols of the faery star and the seaweed — these in a Christian chapel stripped of all Christian symbols. She had been deliberately segregated from the Urquharts — but no expense had been spared for her coffin, and the bronze statue was the work of a master.

An increasing sense of unease gnawed at me.

I felt sure I was missing something. What? One door, one window, and one tomb. What could be missing?

Slowly, thoughtfully, I went back up the steps, closed the ornate gate behind me, locked the seven-point star into place, and went back up the aisle. That was when I spotted the footprints. Footprints in the velvety dust ahead of mine — aimed for vestibule doors.

Someone had walked up the aisle before me.

CHAPTER ELEVEN

The late-afternoon heat was a shock after the damp coolness of the chapel. I locked the doors, thinking rapidly, doing my best to conceal my disquiet from whoever was watching me — for I was sure I was being watched.

I hadn't imagined it. I hadn't imagined my feeling all the long day of being observed, watched. Had Septimus followed me?

Why wouldn't he make himself known?

Could it be Mad Murdo?

But the same argument applied. Why wouldn't he ask what I was doing still poking around the ruins?

Could it be Irania Briggs? I had ditched her in Oban, but she knew I was headed for one of the islands. It was only a matter of time before she figured out which castle I had focused my attention on.

Given the bad reputation of the castle, I had trouble believing another islander or someone on a walking tour had wandered this way.

If this person meant no harm, why didn't he or she speak out?

In any case, there was nothing to observe. I had found Swanhild's tomb and the Urquhart family crypt. There was no sign of the *Faileas a' Chlaidheimh*, and I was all out of ideas.

I had no more leads and no place to go from here.

* * * * *

When I returned to Mrs. Morrison's in time for supper that evening, she informed me Septimus had been recalled to the mainland on urgent business.

I was conscious of a mix of relief — and disappointment.

"When did he go?" I asked.

She gave it thought. "Midmorn, I am thinking."

"Did he happen to say if he would be returning?"

"Aye. He was after telling me he would be back the day after tomorrow." She smiled a motherly sort of smile. "He said you should mind you did not get into trouble."

"Ha," I said feebly, feeling my face warm.

I didn't think there was much chance of my getting into trouble now. I had spent the entire day combing the island estate, and I felt that I had exhausted the possibilities of where the *Faileas a' Chlaidheimh* might be hidden. If it had ever made its way into Swanhild's hands, it had surely disappeared for good after her death.

I spent the evening looking over my notes and my dream journal, but no lead, no clue leaped out at me. It was exactly as I had told Mr. Anstruther and Lady Lavenham at the very beginning. The chances of my uncovering a trail this cold were slim to none.

Feeling discouraged, I turned in early that evening.

And dreamed.

It was a terrifying dream. I woke in the middle of the night drenched in sweat, my heart thundering as though I had been swimming deep, deep below the surface of the ocean and could not make it back to the surface in time before I ran out of oxygen.

In fact, I *had* been dreaming of the ocean. Dreaming of the black and bottomless deep…so vast that leviathans could swim in great pods far below the waves and never be seen at all from the surface. A whole world lay beneath the waves — ancient cities were buried there in the wet darkness, and unknown monsters glided through murky depths.

And fathoms deeper than this, leagues beneath the giant whales and squid and sharks, was still another world as cold and blind as outer space…

It was in that vast midnight nothingness that something stirred, awoke, and opened its red eyes.

That was the dream. A nightmare more like. I fumbled for the lamp, turned it on, and scribbled down what I could remember, and even those unclear recollections had me shivering in the little room with its comfortable bed and cheerful wallpaper.

After I turned the light out once more, I lay there watching the reflection of the sea on the ceiling above me. Silly to react as I had. What was it but an ordinary dream of monsters, and what did monsters represent? A childish resentment of being dominated or the inability to accept and deal with forces beyond my control. It was the dream of the emotionally immature. Even if I erased the monster equation from the dream, dreams about drowning or struggling to stay afloat indicated a subconscious awareness of a need for caution and greater preparation. Wouldn't Septimus love to hear I'd been dreaming of floundering in a deep and terrifying ocean surrounded by monsters?

It was not the dream that was troubling; it was that *I* should have had such a dream.

I was brooding over how inaccurate the dream was, when it suddenly occurred to me that I had overlooked something. Or more precisely, someone. There was a third player in the riddle of the grimoire's disappearance.

Ivan Mago.

The man who had found the *Faileas a' Chlaidheimh* fifty years after it had been lost following the Battle of the Standing Stones. The man who had brought the grimoire back to the island — and been murdered for his trouble.

I had entirely forgotten him. Who was Ivan Mago? An insignificant Scottish conjurer, by all accounts, yet his likeness was in the collection of the Imperial Miniature Society in London.

I had gotten so caught up in the mystery of Swanhild that I'd not even bothered yet to visit the scene of the fatal ambush. It was time to try the puzzle from another angle.

Tomorrow I would do that. Tomorrow I would begin to investigate the murder of Ivan Mago.

* * * * *

The wind howled across the island the next morning, scouring rock and sand and bog. It howled like the black hounds of the Wild Hunt.

First thing, I drove out to Mad Murdo's croft to return his keys. At the last moment I had a change of heart, though, so I told him the key to the castle had fallen off, and I only gave him the main door key. He put it back on the hoop. I waited for him to notice two other keys were still missing, but he seemed quite unaware of anything amiss.

Murdo offered me a dram, which seemed to be common courtesy in these islands, and I accepted with thanks.

As we sipped our whisky, I asked, "Mr. Murdo, do you know anything about the legend concerning a Scottish magician by the name of Ivan Mago?"

Murdo took time lighting his pipe before he answered. "Och, there are a fine lot of legends in these parts, laddie."

"This would be a very old legend. Fourteenth century. Mago was a mainland conjurer who was murdered by island bandits."

He puffed slowly, thoughtfully, and said at last, politely, "That is not a story I am knowing."

That seemed plain enough. I finished my whisky, thanked him, and drove back to the village of Fivepenny Borve, where I had first asked after Agro's castle.

The helpful young woman in the tobacconist shop was behind the counter once more. She smiled broadly in welcome, although her friendliness faded a little when I started asking my questions.

"But it is such an old story. And it is having nothing to do with architecture."

"But since it's so old, what can it matter? No one could be alive now to whom it matters."

"But it matters to you?"

She had me there. I was trying to come up with a reasonable excuse for my nosiness, when she sighed. "Aye, aye. It is an exciting story, true enough. But they were not island bandits that murdered the mainland magician. The Long Island is not a home to bandits."

"Who were they?"

"The soldiers of Agro Urquhart."

"Why would Urquhart's soldiers slay him? Didn't Urquhart's wife ask for him to come to the island?"

"Aye."

"Then why?"

She said noncommittally, "I am thinking Agro Urquhart did not want his wife to be bringing this man to the Long Island."

"Was Ivan Mago her lover?"

She said primly, "That is only something the lady and the gentleman could be knowing for sure."

There it was again: that unnatural caginess about discussing anything to do with Urquhart and the castle. I was sure that it was not my imagination. Everyone I'd spoken to had displayed the same reticence. As though this were recent history and still grounds for giving offense.

Offense to whom? Or what?

I pressed, "Is that the story?"

"It is one story."

"Is there another story?"

"I am only knowing the one story."

"What happened?"

"It was the night of the harvest moon. The soldiers of Urquhart caught the magician from the mainland on the coast road near the druid stone."

"Druid stone?"

"The stone that looks like a chess piece. They killed him and left his body draped on the rock for the eagles."

Lovely. "Did Mago die right away?"

"They say he lived long enough to curse the men who slew him — and the witch who betrayed him."

"*Did* she betray him?"

"No one can be knowing that but the lady herself."

I said carefully, "I suppose the soldiers stripped and robbed him?"

She shook her head, not in negation so much as my guess was as good as hers.

That was the extent of her knowledge. She told me I would know the place where the soldiers caught Mago by the unusual-shaped stone.

"It is not far from the lost village."

"The lost village?"

Her eyes widened a fraction. She looked down at the reddish loose-leaf tobacco she was measuring into glass jars. "Marbost. It is an abandoned village along the coast. There are many like it on the island. Young people do not stay here, and so the old people and the old ways must be dying out eventually."

She was still not meeting my eyes. I thanked her and on impulse bought some of the fragrant tobacco for Septimus.

I set off for the scene of the ambush, slowly driving along the old coast road, keeping an eye out for the stone shaped like a druid or a chess piece. The wind was blowing so hard, the old coupe shook as though we would be knocked into the sea. Electricity crackled in the air.

The land was mostly flat along here. It seemed to me that Mago would have had plenty of time to realize a detail had been sent from the castle. Would he have recognized them as a danger? If he had had time to realize what was happening, would he have tried to prevent the grimoire from falling into the wrong hands?

The coupe crested the small hill, and I saw the stone. It was indeed shaped like a bent and hooded man — very like one of the chess pieces that Mrs. Morrison had set out for Septimus and me two nights ago.

I pulled to the side of the road, got out, and walked the rest of the way. I could see no place along here that Mago might have hidden a book. Unless he had thrown it into the bog nearby. Had he determined that the book was better destroyed than falling into the wrong hands? If so, he had had a lot in common with Septimus and the Vox Pessimires.

I stood for a moment, visualizing it — visualizing Mago as he realized he was being pursued: the distant thunder of horse's hooves, then the scrape and whisper of footsteps on sand, climbing closer, ever closer, the whip of torches in the wind, a smear of yellow in the blackness.

He would know almost at once he was trapped. What would he do? I looked around and spotted a track leading down to the beach.

I followed it until I came to a graveyard in the machair.

Here, there were no fancy, sculpted tombstones or markers as had been in the churchyard on the cliffs. These were plain granite markers. The graves of poor people. Fisherfolk and crofters. I walked among them, studying the inscriptions that had been protected from the relentless Leodhas wind and elements by Old Magick.

The majority of the dates were from around the same era — and no date of death was noted later than 1388.

I stood still, trying to absorb this.

Very well. So the graveyard had fallen out of use after 1388. Not so odd, was it? The girl in the tobacconist shop had said it herself. Young people moved away, and old people died. Villages were abandoned. So, then, would be their graveyards, correct?

I began to examine the gravestones more closely. As the evidence accumulated, the hair rose on the back of my neck. Whole families had died the same year. Man, woman, child. Grandparents and babies. Seventy people all dead the same year.

Was it a plague? A massacre?

The final grave I found was set some distance from the others. There was no name, no inscription. It was a simple stone carved with a crude seven-point star.

I stared at it for some time, suspecting that I was viewing the grave of Ivan Mago.

Or whatever had been left of him after the eagles had finished.

At last I turned and walked back to the sandy track. I followed it down the wildflower-covered hillside to the beach, until I came to what looked to be an abandoned village.

The lost village of Marbost?

I gazed at the crumble of white crofts and broken seawall. A broken chimney rose from the grass and wildflowers.

The graveyard would likely belong to this village — this village that had apparently died in 1388. The same year as Swanhild Somerhairle.

It seemed too great a coincidence.

What connection could this village have to Swanhild? Had the people here tried to offer aid to Ivan Mago? Had they been punished for it? That was the sheerest speculation. Why had Mago come this way, though? Why not the road from Steering Bay? That was the direct route.

I stared out at the little harbor. Mago could have landed here, could have chosen this roundabout way to approach Urquhart's castle, but the only reason for it that I could see would be to conceal his presence on the island.

To conceal his presence from Agro Urquhart.

Success would require the complicity of this village. Why should he have expected that?

But what could have wiped out this entire village if not violent retaliation of some kind? Punishment for a betrayal? Who was better positioned on the island to bring death and destruction to a lot of people at once than the chieftain himself?

I climbed over a broken, blackened wall and dropped down to the spongy ground below, crunching my way over gravel and shell.

Slowly I wandered among the ruins of the lost village. My uneasy suspicion was confirmed. No natural disaster had broken and blackened these stone walls.

I continued down the road until I came to what had clearly been a place of worship. It looked like the ruins of any chapel, but chiseled into the stone threshold was the seven-point star.

So the village of Marbost, like Swanhild, had followed the old religion. Not so surprising. In the fourteenth century, it was Christianity that had been the anomaly. The conversion in Scotland, as in most of the European Alliance states, had been mostly peaceful.

I circled the building, looking for access. I discovered a break in the wall and climbed awkwardly through. The roof was gone, and sunlight shifted across the sand and seaweed-strewn stone floor.

Otherwise the building seemed empty. I was put in mind of the castle chapel. Two places of worship picked clean to the bones of their faith — though the faiths were very different. At least as far as any faith differed one from the other.

Traversing the long room, I heard a whisper behind me — a sound like the scrape of a shoe on a sandy floor. Remembering the alarm of the muniment room the day before, I whirled and saw a shadow standing outlined against the wall. Someone was watching me from just inside the fissure in the wall — someone had climbed in after me.

"Who's there?" I called sharply.

The silhouette moved into the sunlight.

Septimus.

I hadn't realized how alarmed I'd been till I felt the rush of relief.

"You startled me."

"Did I?" Half his face was still in shadow. He seemed unnaturally still.

"Mrs. Morrison said you'd gone back to the mainland."

"I returned this morning."

"Are you following me?" I didn't think he was, so his silence threw me. "*Are* you following me?"

"Yes," he said at last.

"Why?"

"Because I think you're going to find the *Faileas a' Chlaidheimh*."

Well, that made one of us. I wasn't nearly as hopeful. "I thought you didn't want me to find it."

"It doesn't matter what I want. It's too late now."

He sounded grim. I walked toward him, saying, "Look, Septimus, I don't think I'm as close as you believe, but if I was…do you really think I'm so irresponsible that I'd let it go to the highest bidder? If I do find it, I'll take it to the Societas Magicke first. I know the Arcane Services would have to have a say in the disposition of such a powerful grimoire."

He shook his head.

There was something at work here I didn't understand. Something that turned his eyes black with an emotion alarmingly like grief. I put my hand out to him, resting it on his sleeve. "What's wrong?"

He pulled me into his arms, half crushing me, and his mouth found mine. Shockingly I could taste tears on his lips.

I pushed away, staring at him. He was crying. His face was wet, though he made no sound. "What is it? Septimus? What in the name of All is wrong?"

His hands grasped my shoulders hard, then seemed to gentle, sliding down my arms to hold my hands. He gazed gravely into my eyes. His tears had stopped.

"I have to kill you," he said.

"I'm…sorry?" I said what felt like a very long time later.

"Why wouldn't you listen to me?"

"I —"

"I told you, you *must* stop. I warned you it was dangerous, that there were things you didn't comprehend."

"Wait. Let me understand you. You're going to *kill* me?"

"Yes." Septimus sounded weary. He also sounded quite certain. His hands were still closed about my wrists, and I could feel the strength of his grip, though he wasn't hurting me. Yet. "I met yesterday with the presuls of the three separate divisions of the Societas Magicke involved. All were agreed that this was the only course left."

"Wait a minute. *Wait.*" I tried to free myself, and his hands tightened like manacles. "I haven't found it yet. I'm not even close."

"You will find it. It can't be stopped now. You're at the vortex of the gathering forces. The book will surface now. It will reveal itself to you."

"No, it won't. I'll stop the hunt. I'll go home."

"You're still not listening. It's too *late*."

I gave up trying to free myself and said contemptuously, "So the Vox Pessimires don't only destroy books; you're murderers."

"We don't destroy books," Septimus said. "An idea cannot be destroyed. We can only control the humans who use and misuse the power of ideas."

"Control? You mean *kill*?"

"Sometimes. When the stakes are high enough."

"What stakes are so high here?" When he didn't immediately answer, I cried, "If you're going to kill me, Septimus, you at least owe me that."

He drew a harsh breath. "Among the powerful spells in this grimoire are two that cannot be safely shared with the world as it is now."

“What spells?”

“The spell for bringing the dead back to life.”

“But all kinds of spell books claim —”

“And the spell for summoning the most ancient and terrible of all monsters.”

“The end-of-world spell?”

“Yes.”

“But it’s just a legend.”

He shook his head.

“Septimus —” Abruptly, seeing the look in his eyes, I was out of words. I didn’t have an argument against the conviction there. Safe to assume that one didn’t become Vox Pessimires through lack of purpose.

He let go of one of my wrists and rested his hand against my face. I could feel the warmth of his palm against my cheek, feel his light breath against my face, see death in his eyes. I closed my own. I hoped it would not be painful.

I felt rather than saw the shadow that crossed my face as he raised his arm. I said automatically, “Killing me won’t stop the others. And if the *Faileas a’ Chlaidheimh* is about to reveal itself, then all you’re doing by this is cutting yourself from the hunt.”

Nothing happened.

After a moment I unstuck my eyelids and peered cautiously at Septimus. I couldn’t read his expression at all. He was regarding me somberly.

I thought my best chance for survival was to keep my mouth shut now, but I couldn't help it. I said, "Let me find the *Faileas a' Chlaidheimh* and give it to you to dispose of as you think best. If after that, the Societas Magicke still believes I have to die" — I swallowed — "I'll abide by their decision."

The longest five seconds of my life passed before Septimus sighed. "Very well."

"Thank you." My voice shook, but I don't suppose he noticed.

He said a little bitterly, "Don't thank me. I would do nearly anything to spare you. I only hope I'm not choosing your life over all others."

CHAPTER TWELVE

Unsurprisingly conversation was nonexistent between me and Septimus on the drive back to Mrs. Morrison's.

When we reached the former schoolhouse, I turned off the engine and said, "I planned to drive into Steering Bay today to do research in the university library. Have you any objection to that?"

He shook his head. "No. I would ask only that you remember what will happen if you betray my trust."

"How far would I get with the Arcane Services hunting me?" I felt very tired by then. Too tired to drive to Steering Bay, frankly, but I knew that time was running out for me.

We went into the house, and if Mrs. Morrison noticed anything amiss between us, she didn't comment on it.

Over luncheon I asked her about the lost village.

"Och. It will be Marbost you are speaking of." From a large tureen, she dished out bowls of mussel brose, soup made from oatmeal, mussels, and broth.

"Yes. The village by the old graveyard."

She handed me my bowl. "It is an old village, right enough. The story that I heard was that the sea took it."

"The sea? You mean a hurricane or a tidal wave?"

"Aye."

Could the answer be that prosaic? But no, I remembered those blackened and broken walls. It wasn't the sea that had done that.

"Why didn't they rebuild?"

Mrs. Morrison gave me a funny look.

"The other villages rebuilt, didn't they? The sea couldn't have taken one village alone."

"That is the story I was told."

An answer that was not an answer. Interesting. I asked, "Where was the sea witch born?"

In the pause that followed, Mrs. Morrison carefully dished out soup into Septimus's bowl. "She is coming from Marbost," she said at last, and her accent seemed unusually strong.

I glanced at Septimus. He raised his brows.

* * * * *

The university library at Steering Bay was large and well organized, but despite its proximity to the island, it had no more information on Agro Urquhart or Swanhild Somerhairle than the libraries of London. What it did have was a full-size oil portrait of Swanhild in the rare-documents room.

I gazed at the portrait, fascinated, for nearly a full half an hour.

The sketch I had seen at the Museum of the Literary Occult had not given a true picture of her beauty or youth. Her hair was red, not dark. A rich red like the pelt of a fox. Her eyes were green — as green as Septimus's. The delicate beauty of her bone structure did not seem quite human. I wondered again if there was something fey in her bloodline, though she had been painted in the traditional fashion: green velvet gown and Scottish deerhounds at her side. I could see why Agro Urquhart had fallen in love with her at first sight.

When I had gleaned what I could from the portrait, I went in search of someone who could translate the meaning of the Gaelic inscription on Urquhart's statue. One of the librarians took the slip of paper, read it over, and then read it again. He gave me a quizzical look.

"This is grim stuff. It says, 'We have not lost our way. Our way has lost us.' Where is it from?"

"An old gravestone."

"Doesn't sound like the current tenant was entertaining much hope for a happy afterlife."

"No, it doesn't," I agreed, taking the paper and folding it up again.

Having already exhausted the resources of the university library, I headed for High Street, walking unseeingly past shops and pubs and cafés. It had occurred to me that, although Septimus and I had not discussed this option, failure to find the grimoire would probably lead to my death as surely as finding it would.

What if I did try running? What if I fled the island and booked passage back to the Americas? To the safety of Boston and Blackie's Books.

But I knew the answer to that. Septimus said he had consulted the three presuls involved. One of them would have been my own kindly Mr. Phillips. Kindly Mr. Phillips who had apparently concurred that the world would be safer with me dead.

There was nowhere to run, and if I tried and was caught — which I almost certainly would be with the Arcane Services hunting me — I'd be all out of chances. No, my best bet was to control my fear and focus on finding the grimoire. If I could find it, handing it over immediately — rather than using it to try and protect myself — would be my surest means of convincing Septimus and those he reported to that I was no danger.

I stopped at a pub to drown my sorrows in a quick pint, then telefoned Dr. Spindrift in Oban. The doctor's maid informed me the doctor was still napping.

Another dead end.

Next on my list was Mr. Anstruther at the Museum of the Literary Occult. I needed to apprise him of the situation; I owed him that much. I resisted the temptation to fortify myself with another pint.

Mr. Anstruther came on the line breathing fire and brimstone. "So you've finally decided to check in, Mr. Bliss! I suppose you're running short of funds?"

I said, subdued, "No. I'm all right for money —"

"And while you're spending my money, what progress have you made, may I ask?"

His hostility sidetracked my determination to make a clean breast of things. "Not a great deal. I warned you at the start it wouldn't be easy — that it might not be possible."

"Where are you now?"

"Steering Bay. I've been to the university library."

"Never mind the university! What about the castle? What about the sea caves? What have you found there?"

I started to answer but cut myself off. Instead I said, "How do you know about the sea caves?" More, how did he know I'd already been to the castle? Belatedly suspicious, I asked, "Have you hired someone else to find the — it." I remembered the first time Anstruther had mentioned Irania Briggs. I'd had a fleeting sense then that I'd heard her name before. But where? When? It still eluded me.

I looked uneasily over my shoulder, but no one in the pub seemed to pay me any mind. No face looked familiar.

Anstruther said irascibly, "What if I have? It's my money. Why shouldn't I hedge my bets? I'm still paying you a pretty penny."

"Who did you hire?"

"I've told you all you need to know. Now, what have you discovered? And don't give me that nonsense about not finding anything, for I know you've discovered *something*."

"I don't understand. Why do you want this book so desperately?"

"Why wouldn't I want this book? What is there to understand? Why wouldn't any book collector want this book? The *Faileas a' Chlaidheimh* may well be the greatest of the great grimoires."

"You do realize how dangerous it is?"

"Who have you been talking to?" Anstruther demanded. "No, don't tell me. I know. It's that bloody Magister Marx again, isn't it?"

I saw no point in lying about it now. "Yes." Marx's interest was probably the closest thing I had to an insurance policy.

"Don't believe anything he tells you!"

"Why would he lie?"

"Because the Societas Magicke wants to possess and control all the magickal texts in the world. They want to prevent the rest of us from having access to the magick that could even save our lives."

I had it then. I knew what the elderly and frail Anstruther was after. Immortality.

I lowered my voice in case anyone was listening in. "Even if it's true. Even if *The Sword's Shadow* can restore life to the dead, you can't use Old Magick like that. You can't introduce it back into the world without…without safeguards."

"What do you know of it? Wait till you're my age, till you're old and ill, till you're crippled and dying, and tell me then that you won't use any means to preserve your life." He added with sudden venom, "Or to destroy anyone who stands between you and the only chance you have."

Well, that was patent enough — and it was time to place my cards on the table. "I can't help you any longer, Mr. Anstruther. Not with this. It was one thing when I thought you wished only to preserve the book, but to use it —"

"Of course I plan to use it. What use is it otherwise? It was created for that purpose."

"I'm sorry, but I have to resign this commission."

In the silence that fell between us, I could hear the friendly *clink* of glasses and the cheerful murmur of voices behind me.

"I wouldn't do that, Mr. Bliss," Anstruther said almost cordially. "If you attempt to double-cross me, I'll see that you are made very, *very* sorry."

"You've no idea how very, very sorry I already am, Mr. Anstruther." I hung up the telefon.

I left the pub and continued on my way up High Street, but I no longer walked with any purpose. It was hard to think how matters could possibly get any worse. Other than being slain by Septimus. That would certainly be worse.

A tall, slender figure in gray silk passed me, reflected in the plate-glass window. My gaze sharpened, and I glanced over my shoulder.

Surely I knew that walk? And how many women in the Scottish isles were wearing London fashions. Then again, if the faery folk were wearing London fashions…

I was still puzzling over these thoughts when the woman turned and gazed at me over her shoulder. She wore a sheer white veil, but I could see her face quite clearly. Her red-brown eyes seemed to burn into my own. I saw her mouth form a word.

At first I thought she said *magick*. Then I realized it was a name. *Mago.*

The next moment she had turned the corner. I turned to follow, but when I rounded the corner, there was no sign of her.

I looked about. In my pursuit of the faery woman, I had dived down a side street. It seemed quite empty, not a tourist or sightseer anywhere. I stood in front of a small brick shop. The windows were tinted. At least, I couldn't see into the shop. A dark wood sign hung over the door. Painted in red and blue were the words MAGO & MAGO.

I stepped inside. It smelled of incense and furniture polish. As my eyes adjusted to the dim light, I saw that the shop was crammed floor to ceiling with old furniture and junk. A brownie was busily dusting brass candlesticks. Behind the counter, a small man was sitting very still on a tall stool.

"Hello," I said.

"Will you come in?" His voice was English and educated—public school, I thought. He sounded like Antony. It occurred to me with some relief that it had been quite a while since I'd spared Antony a thought. Granted, I had bigger problems than Antony these days.

"May I look around?"

The man behind the counter nodded gravely.

I browsed the shelves, but my attention was all on the man sitting so very still on his stool. Now that I had a better look at him, I realized he probably wasn't human. Or not completely. The thinning hair was only too human, but his hands were very tiny, and his wizened features were more those of a hobgoblin or perhaps a dwarf, although there were not many dwarves in Scotland.

As I inspected snuffboxes and perfume bottles, he closed his eyes, seeming to show no interest. I moved on to the bookshelves. He had a small but select offering of titles. Finally I picked up a volume of nineteenth-century love poems and moved to the counter.

"Are you Mr. Mago?"

His eyes opened. The blue irises were ringed in black. Most definitely not human. "There is no Mr. Mago. I am Mr. Saltin. I bought the shop from the last Mr. Mago, oh, many years ago now."

"I wondered because I've been researching a Mr. Ivan Mago."

"Ah."

"The fourteenth-century Mr. Mago," I clarified.

"There was only one Mr. Ivan Mago."

"Do you know if he —"

"Yes."

That seemed firm. "Could you tell me about him?"

Mr. Saltin's pencil-thin eyebrows rose. "What would you know, old chap?"

"Anything, really. Who was he?"

The tiny hands raised. "You see."

"A dealer of antiquities." I said tentatively, "And magick?"

"Old Magick." Saltin shrugged. "Not much call for that these days."

"Was he…veneficus?"

"Oh yes. They all were, the Magos. A long line of magicians and conjurers."

I said tentatively, "He apparently came to a violent end."

"He was murdered." Saltin smiled a tight-lipped smile. "It can be a dangerous trade, antiquities."

"I've heard a lot of stories."

"There are a bloody lot of stories," he agreed. "Odd. No one asks about Ivan Mago, and yet this week I've had two callers."

I stared. "Who else asked about Mago?"

"A *beautiful* young lady from London. Don't get many beautiful young ladies in our shop, I'm afraid." He winced as the brownie's duster knocked a tall candlestick off the shelf. It crashed to the floor.

"Did she give a name?"

"No." He gave another of those tight smiles. "Ours is not a trade for names."

"What did she look like?"

Mr. Saltin described in loving detail what she had looked like. Irania Briggs was gaining on me — in fact, she'd been two steps ahead in finding this place.

"Can I ask what she wanted of you?"

"She asked me how a powerful grimoire like the *Faileas a' Chlaidheimh* could fall into the hands of a man like Ivan Mago."

At the name of the grimoire, the lights in the shop, already low, flickered and then went dark. They flared on almost immediately and illuminated Mr. Saltin laughing soundlessly at me.

I asked steadily, "What did you tell her?"

He stopped laughing and shrugged. "Why, I told her the truth. These things happen."

* * * * *

It was late when I parked in front of Mrs. Morrison's. The moon shone brightly in the purple night. The downstairs lights of the schoolhouse were shining in welcome as I walked up the shell-strewn path. Through the open windows, I could smell homely smells of cooking and the fragrance of a pipe.

Septimus opened the door to me. "I was beginning to think you'd tried to run after all."

I said wearily, "How far would I get?"

"Not far." He drew me over the threshold and into his arms. His mouth was quite tender as he found mine — that tenderness seemed the strangest thing that had happened all day.

I pulled back out of his arms and said, "Where is Mrs. Morrison?"

"There's a *ceilidh* in the village. Have you eaten?"

I shook my head.

Septimus led the way to the kitchen, and I sat down at the table and watched him carve a wedge of meat pie and put it on a plate for me.

"Maybe you shouldn't bother. You may have to kill me sooner than expected."

He laid the plate in front of me and took the chair across the table. His face looked older, as though he had aged since that morning. I was abruptly reminded of that gaunt, hollow-eyed portrait of Agro Urquhart that I had seen in the Museum of the Literary Occult. The portrait painted near the end of his life.

Septimus stated, “I know colonials have their own sense of humor, but I can’t joke about this.”

“If you’ll notice, I’m not laughing.”

“You’re not eating either.” He nodded to the plate.

I snorted, picked up my fork, and began to eat. After the first bite, I recognized I was much hungrier than I’d realized. Septimus rose, left the room, and returned with two glasses of whisky. He placed one beside my plate, then sat down again and lit his pipe.

For a time neither of us spoke. All things considered, it was strangely peaceful in that little island kitchen.

At length, I pushed my empty plate aside and took a good swallow of whisky. It burned comfortingly all the way down my throat. I had another swallow.

I put my glass down and said, “Why did Agro Urquhart slay his wife?”

“That much you already know.”

I nodded. “She betrayed him.”

“Yes.”

“But not through adultery?”

“That, he could have forgiven.”

I said, watching his face, “She followed the old ways. She was half-Sodreys and resented Urquhart and his new religion. But he fell in love and wanted her anyway — and he took her.”

“Yes.”

"But one day she received word that the *Faileas a' Chlaidheimh* had been found, and she sent for it."

Septimus stretched his arm to me. "Give me your hand."

Cautiously I placed my hand in his. I saw it all then…like moving pictures in the cinema sliding past, like a reversed perusing. I saw a young girl standing on a cliffside staring out to sea, a young girl with red hair and wide green eyes. I felt her bitterness at the marriage she did not want — more than that. Anger at the way her world was changing, the abandonment of the old gods and the old ways… The pictures wavered, and I saw a man in a shop that looked nearly unchanged from the shop I had stood in that very day. A quiet, lonely man, a scholar, a man only too ready to fall in love with this fierce, beautiful girl. And I saw the tentative courtship spring up through modes of magick so antiquated, I barely recognized them. Scrying bowls and casting runes — primitive stuff. Primitive but effective. I saw this man wrapping a great golden book and setting off on his final journey…

The picture faded, and I became aware that I was sitting in Mrs. Morrison's kitchen holding Septimus's hand. His fingers were long and thin, but very strong — gentle too. I wondered why I hadn't trusted him before. When there had still been time to set things right.

I pulled my hand free. "How did you do that?"

"It's a skill learned like any other."

"That's not like any magick I've seen in the service."

"It's unique to the Vox Pessimires."

"Like murder."

I hadn't meant to say it. His face closed. He said, "Say execution, rather."

"It's actually funny. We're all so appalled at the idea that the Vox Pessimires destroy books."

"Don't." Septimus rose, the chair scraping noisily back. "I warned you, Colin. I told you, you must stop. You wouldn't listen."

"You should've told me the truth. I'd have certainly stopped if I'd realized you'd kill me if I didn't."

"Colin."

He spoke with such anguish, I fell silent.

Septimus's voice sounded thick as he said, "I love you. Do you not understand that? If it were possible, I'd die in your place."

"No." I was surprised how quickly the word slipped out, how much I didn't want that sacrifice — couldn't bear to think of it.

Astonished, I turned that revelation over and examined it from all sides. Now that was one for the books, as we say in the service. The supreme idiocy: I'd fallen in love with my executioner.

Listening to Septimus struggle to control the harshness of his breathing, the emotion threatening to tear out of him — and beyond, the ordinary night sounds drifting in through the open window, an unexpected calm washed over me.

I rose and went to him, slipped my arms around his lean waist and rested my face against the back of his head. The long, dark strands smelled sweet. I kissed the back of his neck, and he shivered.

"Let's spend what time we can together."

He turned to me, his brows drawing together, giving him a devilish aspect. He looked, more than anything, wary.

It struck me as mildly funny. I said, "I don't want to be alone now. Is that so strange?"

"No."

I couldn't meet his eyes, didn't want to see that expression now. I took his hand and led the way up the stairs to the room with the big brass bed and old-fashioned wallpaper.

We undressed in the soft lamplight and came together.

The other times our coupling had been frenzied, near-delirious; this was tranquil by comparison. We eased back down into the cloud of bedding. I settled my hips against the warmth of his groin. He stroked and petted me until I could have purred like the cat did beneath his ministrations. There was that familiar bright flash of pain that faded swiftly in the wake of always startling pleasure. I pushed back, Septimus rocked forward, and we began to move into a rhythm that grew less awkward and more pleasurable with every thrust.

The blankets and duvet puffed gently around us like breaths — mimicking our own increasingly erratic gasps and groans. I reached up and grabbed the brass bars of the headboard to give myself more leverage. Septimus shifted, thrust harder, and the bedsprings shrieked excitedly. My entire body clenched, every muscle drawing tight, and that shimmering starting to tingle from the root of my cock to the tip.

Oh there was no magick like this, like this white-hot sparkling fountain shooting up into the gentle darkness. I could feel Septimus sliding in and out right under my heart, and climax rolled through like a great tide.

Afterward we lay in locked in each other's arms. Somewhere in the distance I could hear the eerie sound of bagpipes. The village ceilidh must be ending.

I whispered, "You never said. Did you find your eleventh-century Unseelie Court encyclopedia?"

"No." He added reluctantly, "This took precedence."

"This?"

He gave a ghost of a laugh, slowly carding my curls between his fingers.

"I saw her today."

"Who?"

"Your faery lady."

Septimus stopped stroking my hair. I could feel the depth of his silence echoing all around us.

"What do you mean?" he asked at last.

"The faery woman. The one you spoke to that day you left my office. When we were in London."

Far from clarifying matters, I seemed to be bewildering Septimus more with each sentence. "You saw that? You saw — What did you see?"

"I saw you speak to her. I saw her disappear."

"You *saw* her?" He couldn't seem to get over it.

"I've seen her a few times."

"You've —" He rolled away from me and turned on the light. He was staring at me as though he'd never seen me before. "When?"

"The first time was after I met with Anstruther and Lady Lavenham. I saw her today as well."

"Today?"

"When I was in Steering Bay. She pointed out Mago's shop to me."

He opened his mouth, but no sound came out. He continued to stare at me as though I'd transformed into something fantastical right before his eyes.

"What is it?"

He swallowed. "Why didn't you say something?"

"I was a little distracted," I pointed out. "Why is this so shocking to you?"

He shook his head and continued to eye me in that unnerving way. "Don't you know?" he inquired finally.

"No."

"If the Seelie Court is guiding you —" He broke off.

"I wouldn't say she's guiding me. She's just appeared a few times."

Septimus seemed at a loss. "Colin…don't you see? This changes everything."

"For better or worse?"

"I don't know." He snapped out the light and stretched down beside me once more. When he put his arm around me, it seemed almost tentative. "When was the last time you were tested?"

"For what?"

"Aptitude in the occult sciences."

"When I enlisted, I suppose. We don't really test like y —"

His kiss stopped me. We were both breathless when he raised his head at last.

"Not that I didn't enjoy it, but what was that for?"

"We'll talk about it later. We should sleep now." He pulled the duvet up over my shoulders, tucking it more warmly about me.

CHAPTER THIRTEEN

Septimus was sleeping when I slipped out from under his arm and dressed quickly and quietly in a patch of moonlight. As much as I wanted his help, I was not sure he could give it without fatally compromising himself. I didn't want that — couldn't contemplate it. He was quite right. I had brought this all on myself. I couldn't allow him to pay the price for my folly.

When I glanced back at the bed, his face was silvered and remote in sleep. I resisted the temptation to kiss him.

I crept downstairs. Mrs. Morrison had returned home at some point while we slept. The front door was barred.

I unlocked it and stepped outside, then eased the door closed and ran lightly to the coupe. Sounds carried in the clear night air, so I was very cautious opening and closing the door.

I released the brake and let it roll silently down the hillside, tires crunching on sand and rock. When it neared the bottom, I turned on the engine and lights and headed back to the little island.

By now I knew the way well enough to find the path across the uneven pasture by moonlight. Even lugging the parcel of equipment I'd purchased in Steering Bay, I moved swiftly. I made it across the bridge and through the woods in record time.

The knowledge that Irania Briggs and her mysterious ally were gaining on me had solidified my conviction that there was no time to be lost in locating the *Faileas a' Chlaidheimh*. There were only two places left I could think of to try: the sea caves and the muniment room. If I hadn't found the sea caves in the day, I was unlikely to find them at night, so that exploration would have to wait, but I could explore the muniment room at night as easily as any other time. The ledgers there had to be examined underground and in darkness either way.

Unseen things rustled in the undergrowth as I let myself in through the gate, which screeched an alarm I was sure could be heard all the way to the Long Island.

I pushed my way through the vines and brush to the marble archway. There I knelt and shone my torch until I found the keyhole.

The nearby rattling *crex-crex* of a corncrake had me nearly jumping out of my skin. My skittering flashlight beam fell on the sinuous carvings in the marble column: the crested snake. I leaned closer to see.

My scalp prickled as at last I realized what that emblem was. Not a snake. A serpent. A sea serpent. The greatest of all sea serpents — of all monsters — the Cirein-cròin.

I rocked back on my heels, absorbing it.

Of course. It seemed so obvious now. What else *would* it be in this forsaken corner of the Old World? No wonder Septimus and the rest of the Societas Magicke were in a panic.

Cirein-cròin.

The great beast of the ocean. Also known as the great whirlpool of the ocean, the monster of the ocean, and the death of the world.

Legend held it was the largest animal to ever live. There was even an old children's rhyme:

Seven herring are a salmon's fill

Seven salmon are a seal's fill,

Seven seals are a whale's fill,

And seven whales, the fill of a Cirein-cròin.

My hand was shaking as I unlocked the round door to the muniment room and dragged it back. I went quickly down the steps and ran for the underground chamber.

What followed would have horrified most librivenators and librireddos alike, for I did not read so much as ransack the shelves of ledgers in the small chamber.

Beginning with the latest date, I worked steadily backward, sifting contents methodically, leaving no book or document untouched or unopened. When I came to the ledgers for the year 1388, I scanned them quickly before setting them aside in a stack to go through more carefully, time permitting.

Time being something none of us might have.

Some of the oldest books, those of the Sodreys lords, were bound in bulky iron frames, almost too heavy to lift. The rucked parchment pages of unglazed paper were brittle and yellow. They crumbled beneath my rough handling. For once I didn't care. What use was protecting a few historical documents if the world itself died?

I pored over deeds, grants, marriage contracts, and warrants of good condition. What Basil wouldn't give for this collection in its entirety or even in part. Even in my haste, I knew how valuable was this page-by-page documentation of bygone life, the life of the wealthy and privileged. My fingers flew past bills for beef and wine and candle wax.

You could have tracked every meal for a year if you were so inclined.

The Sodreys lords had been warlike, but no less had been Agro Urquhart.

The ledgers from 1386 onward amounted primarily to staggering bills for a war chest; soldiers and weapons did not come cheap, even in the 1300s. And then in the browned pages of 1387, I found the listing of marriage expenses. Swanhild had brought no dowry to the marriage. No love either.

Agro Urquhart's passion had cost him dearly.

I worked for several hours before my torch began to fade. By then I had already determined that the *Faileas a' Chlaidheimh* was not concealed between the covers of any other ledger.

The stuffiness of the chamber made my head swim.

I staggered down the low tunnel, crawled up the steps, and collapsed on a prickly patch of grass and heather. Empty and exhausted, I stared up at the yellow moon drifting through the loosely threaded night clouds. The two marble columns seemed to tilt above me, limned in golden light.

The persistent *Leòdhas* wind sketched through the grass and leaves, sending them fluttering in panic.

Abruptly the breeze died, and all was still and strange.

I was missing something. Something obvious.

Into that windless silence I heard the familiar melodious song of a woodland thrush singing its good-night air. Tears filled my eyes at the sweetness of that hopeful sound.

I mustn't give up now. Reluctantly I dragged myself to my feet and returned to the muniment room and the stack of ledgers from 1388.

It would have been in the summer... I was sure I'd read that somewhere...or did I just feel that truth? Book hunter's instinct perhaps. I searched through the summer months for accounts that would give me some clue into the days surrounding the witch's death.

In the month of August, I found the commission for a black marble tomb.

Staring at the impersonal figures, I felt a growing tension, an unease.

I closed my eyes to peruse and nearly dropped the ledger at the whirlwind of images that slammed into me.

I could see her as though she sat a few feet from me. A girl of seventeen, perhaps, sitting in a dark cave. Her red hair was spilled and loose over her shoulders; her eyes glinted like the wet shining on the craggy walls of her prison. There was a scrape on her cheekbone, and she cradled her arm as though it was broken. She was listening, and when the earth shook, she smiled...

I saw the man come for her. Saw him silhouetted in the mouth of the cave — saw her put a hand up, her eyes dazzled by the daylight — saw him drag her out and draw his sword…

I clapped the ledger shut and leaned weakly against the wall of the chamber.

My perusals were growing stronger, more vivid…the line between past and present blurring. For all the good it did. I scrubbed my eyes and tried to think. I was so desperately tired by then…

I wished for Septimus. Not merely his companionship, although that would have been welcome, but his experience and knowledge in these matters.

There had been no grimoire in the sea cave with Swanhild; she'd have used it if it had been there, of that I had no doubt. So it had been lost to her even before then? If that was the case, what chance did I have of finding it now?

I dropped my head in my hands, flooded by a sense of the hopelessness of the task before me.

Had I really explored every route? Every possibility? What about my feeling in the witch's tomb of something puzzling and inexplicable?

Yes. There was something there. I was sure of it. There was no solving this without another visit to the chapel and the secluded tomb.

I pushed away from the wall and climbed out of the tunnel once more. The wind had picked up. It was playing a deep and dire organ sound in the billowing treetops overhead. The sky had faded to an eerie green-black like an upside-down vision into the sea.

I shouldered the parcel of tools I had purchased in Steering Bay, and set off through the wind-tossed jungle.

* * * * *

The chapel doors opened with an unearthly howl — but it was only rusty hinges, nothing of the veneficus. I went through the swinging doors, which also screeched in welcome, and shone my increasingly feeble torch at the footsteps in the dust.

Many footsteps now. Someone had been in and out of the chapel since my last trip.

Septimus? He had admitted he had been following me. I remembered that first day exploring the muniment chamber — my fear that I would be sealed into that tomb of old papers and ledgers. Had that been an instinct of real danger? Had Septimus considered locking me in that afternoon?

I shivered and continued down the aisle to the gated passageway.

This time I had no trouble opening the gate. I shoved aside the grating and went swiftly down the staircase to the tomb.

The bronze statue's smile flickered from the shadows.

Agro Urquhart had been a simple man. Not foolish. Simple as in straightforward. He was a man of contradictions, a man of violent passions. A man who could fall in love at first sight with a fish gutter — slay her when she betrayed him — and commission a tomb fit for a queen. As a warrior, he would have understood both risk and expediency.

What would such a man do if he found himself the untimely possessor of the most powerful book of spells in all the world? He would destroy it, wouldn't he? But perhaps that wasn't possible. Everyone who would know seemed certain the grimoire had survived. I had always believed such works were destructible, but that was when I had believed the Vox Pessimires were capable of expunging magickal texts. That turned out to be false, so perhaps the rumors were true and such a book had wards to protect it?

If it wasn't possible to destroy the book? What then?

Presented with the most dangerous book of spells in the world, what would a practical man like Urquhart do? I thought that he might very well lay the book to rest with the witch who had tried to use it against him. What surer hiding place for the *Faileas a' Chlaidheimh* than the tomb of Swanhild Somerhairle?

I lowered my sack of tools to the stone floor. The effigy itself was hollow, but even so it would not be an easy task to get the lid up. That slab of marble was likely four or five hundred pounds.

I knelt and quickly unpacked the things I had bought after leaving Mago's shop: a powerful standing lantern, a couple of spikes and mallets, two crowbars, and an assortment of chocks and wedges. I had expected to use these things in exploring the sea caves, but they would serve just as well here.

I lit the lantern, and harsh white light flooded the room. The tomb and bronze statue seemed to spark with glints of reds, blues, and gilt against black marble. The weather-stained walls looked like blood, shining slick and bright.

Picking up one of the crowbars, I considered what I was about to do. An unexpected weakness filled me. If the grimoire *was* here, was I making a last and fatal mistake by retrieving it?

But how could I stop now? Irania Briggs and her mysterious cohort were right on my heels. Better for me to find the grimoire and hand it over to Septimus than to leave it for them, surely?

I froze at the sound of a surreptitious footfall. Going to the mouth of the chamber, I gripped the crowbar and stared up at the winding staircase.

The sound came again…and then again. I relaxed. The steady repetition told me it was only a drip of water from the roof striking the marble floor. The heavy, regular pulse was amplified by the acoustics of the high, echoing vault ceiling.

I returned to the black marble tomb and stared down. Even if my curiosity and stubbornness hadn't insisted that I see this through, it was too late now. I had brought attention to the chapel, and if the grimoire was in here, it was only a matter of time before my rivals in this quest discovered it. Squeamishness would not keep Irania from opening the tomb. Of that I was confident.

On second thought, I set the crowbar aside, picked up a spike, and wedged the tip beneath the black marble lid, using the mallet to tap my way down the line of mortar that sealed the lid. Dust from the mortar floated up. I sneezed, wiped my face, and proceeded down the length of the tomb. I needed only do three sides of the box.

It took only a short while to chip the seal completely away, revealing a perfectly even hairline crack. Unfortunately that gave no point of leverage, no widening of the fissure at any point where I could work the crowbar in without destroying the lid. If I was wrong, I was desecrating a tomb for no good cause. Even if I was right, I had now officially entered the profession of grave robbing. The observation did little to inspire me.

I rested for a minute, listening to the clockwork beat of water hitting stone at the top of the stairs. It did sound amazingly like a firm footstep walking from the past into the present.

I shrugged off my nerves, picked up the spike once more, and placed it against the crack midway on the long side of the tomb. I hit it once sharply with the mallet. The blow echoed through the chamber with reverberation like a thudding footstep.

A few seconds later, black and gilt slivers lay on the floor. The crack displayed a gaping underlip about an inch long and quarter inch wide, with a slight fracturing of glossy marble beneath. The damage was not obvious damage to the naked eye, which was some comfort, and I now had space sufficient to my purpose.

I bore down with the crowbar, inserting it into the crack.

Nothing happened.

Was there another seal that I couldn't see? Some trick of ancient engineering?

I changed angle and pitched my strength against it. I had completely underestimated the weight of what I was trying to shift.

The combined mass might of marble and bronze probably weighed half a ton.

No single man could budge this. It would take two — maybe three.

I rested and tried to think of ways to lever and use the weight of the lid to shift it. I would have to get help. I'd have to go to Septimus after all. The idea filled me with relief. Yes, let Septimus take some of the responsibility for this. He was better equipped to make these kinds of decisions.

I stood there listening to the *drip, drip* of the ceiling, steady and somehow lifeless, and another sound impinged on my consciousness. I listened more closely, and I realized the measured beat was *not* water. Footsteps separated themselves from the other sounds. Footsteps were coming my way.

Septimus had followed me.

That was what I told myself, tried to reassure myself, but my sense of unease grew as I waited, listening to the footsteps coming slowly, steadily toward me.

CHAPTER FOURTEEN

He came rapidly down the rest of the steps and appeared in the doorway: tall, middle-aged, sandy haired. Antony.

"She planned to bring back the Sodreys gods and rid the isle of Urquhart. Imagine that! Quite ambitious, wasn't it? One of Urquhart's female lieutenants got word of what Swanhild planned, and warned him. His men ambushed Mago and killed him. But one of Swanhild's island men was among Urquhart's soldiers. He found the grimoire and brought it to her."

He spoke in that lecturing, slightly pompous voice, and I realized the poor light had deceived me — or my eyes were playing tricks. It was Basil.

And he was holding a revolver. It was pointed at me.

I had a sudden memory of standing in Basil's office, watching him opening an envelope addressed in brown ink. So here was the expert with whom Anstruther and Lavenham had decided to "hedge their bets." Of course. Basil was an obvious choice.

He continued in that same instructional tone. "When Urquhart came for her, Swanhild summoned the Cirein-cròin. Well, adolescent girls. It's not surprising, is it? But she really wasn't a very good witch. She lost control of the monster, and it took down the tower with her in it. Somehow she survived, and Urquhart recovered the grimoire and had her imprisoned in the sea caves."

My mouth was desert dry. I unstuck my tongue from the roof of my mouth and asked, "What happened to the Cirein-cròin?"

"Oh, it proceeded to wreak devastation all along the coast, as you might expect. Finally, in a last-ditch effort to stop it, Urquhart slew Swanhild and had her buried in the chapel. The Cirein-cròin vanished and has never been seen since."

"Nor the grimoire," I said.

"Well, that at least is about to change, isn't it?" He gestured with the pistol. "What are you waiting for?"

"I can't shift it on my own. I don't even know if it's really in here."

"Oh, you know." There was a note of bitterness in his voice. "You have quite a gift, Mr. Bliss. Marx was right about that."

I didn't move a muscle. "What does Marx have to do with this?"

Basil smiled. "I'm sure he's told you by now. He's been agonizing over it since he discovered what you were up to. Even Antony was mildly depressed to sign your death warrant. But I expect that's mostly at the idea of filling out the new personnel-request forms. *You* wanted to be a librivenator. This is the price you pay." He waved the pistol at me.

"I can't move this on my own. It probably weighs half a ton."

He studied the tomb. "It probably does. How very like you to hope to tackle it on your own." He shoved the revolver into his waistband. "All right. You stay at that end. If you try to jump me, I'll shoot you. Don't make any mistake about that."

"Basil, you know better than anyone how dangerous th —"

"*Eesht* or whatever it is they say on this godforsaken island." He bent toward the second crowbar but paused. "There might be a trap inside. Had you thought of that?"

"Trap?" No, I hadn't thought of that.

"Granted, fourteenth century is a bit late for that kind of thing." Basil regarded the tomb thoughtfully and then me. "What a face! We did try to warn you that it's different on this side of the Great Big Sea." He bent again, picked up the crowbar.

"How did you know to find me?"

He chuckled. "It wasn't hard at all. There's a book in the imperial library with the entire legend if you'd bothered to look." Glancing around, he said, "Wedges. Good. Very practical. Be ready when the lid comes up. And remember: it won't take me half a mo to drop the crowbar and shoot you between those wide eyes of yours."

He buckled to the job with expertise and strength, while I used the other crowbar to apply leverage.

A long black gap appeared beneath the lid, and the bronze girl tilted backward.

"Hang on," he ordered, and he stooped to grab the first of the wedges.

Ten minutes later we were done. The wall behind the tomb had caught the tilting mass and prevented it from opening fully, but I'd brought enough chocks that even with the obstacle of the wall, a long strip of darkness somewhat more than a foot deep showed beneath the wedged lid.

We were silent, staring at each other. I'd be lying if I tried to deny my heart was pounding with excitement. Here was the end of the chase, and I was too much of a book hunter not to be caught up in the moment.

"Go on, then," Basil said after a pause. He motioned me forward. "It's only fair that the honor goes to you." He handed me the torch.

With unsteady hands, I turned the flashlight on and shone it inside the midnight slit. My excitement gave way to instinctive, animal dread of the dead. Up until now it had all been rather academic. The stuff of legends and myth. Even the perusing was more like watching cinema than reliving the past.

I leaned down and felt revulsion as a faint charnel whiff rose out of the marble box — not a scent, maybe the ghost of a scent.

"Go on," Basil said impatiently. "Squeamish, are you? Surely not, the way you've been picking over the bones of the past."

I shouldered my hesitation aside and put my head beneath the lid into the cold nastiness of the illumined marble box. I looked down.

Eyes looked up into my own.

I recoiled, banging my head hard on the marble lid. Stars swam before my eyes. I hung on to the edge of the tomb and blinked them away.

"What is it?" Basil demanded. And when I couldn't seem to find the words to answer, "What the devil is wrong with you?"

"She's —" I pulled back out and stared at him.

He scowled. "She's what? This had better not be a trick."

I shook my head. He snatched the flashlight out of my hand. "Stand over there."

I moved over to the corner — unfortunately well out of range of my being able to grab him.

Basil threw me one last suspicious glance and ducked beneath the lid himself.

After a long, paralyzed moment, he emerged speechless. But unlike me, he recovered at once and got in motion, first measuring the opening with a glance, then once more thrusting his head in and reaching downward, his back and shoulders straining at the awkward position.

In a few moments he withdrew his head again and, with his arms held stiffly before him, carefully brought out what at first appeared to be a log of driftwood from between the marble jaws. He laid it carefully on the floor. He rose.

Unspeaking, we stared down at it, at the mummified remains clutching the book, which shone like a star in the drab cell.

"'Its cover made of beaten gold as thin as paper and inlaid with mother-of-pearl and cairngorms plucked from the bowels of the purple mountains.'" I remembered Mr. Anstruther's words that long-ago afternoon in the Museum of the Literary Occult.

My gaze moved in revolted fascination to the remains of Swanhild Somerhairle.

She had been tall for a girl. Her hair, which looked like red and fraying ropes, was down to her waist. Her skin had hardened and cured like leather or parchment so that her face was no mere skull, but recognizably a face.

Even in the short interim since we had opened the tomb, her eyes had vanished. She was crumbling away to nothing even as we looked.

Basil knelt to lift the grimoire from her arms, which broke away. I sucked in a horrified breath and instinctively moved forward. Basil pulled his revolver and shot me.

The deafening blast was still ricocheting around the stone chamber as, hand clapped to my shoulder, I slid down the wall. I stared at him in disbelief. My left arm felt like lead. Dead. There was a tiny jerking fountain of blood coming from the hole in my shoulder.

"What did you do that for?" I asked stupidly.

"I warned you not to try anything."

On the floor next to the remains of Swanhild, the heavy gold cover of the *Faileas a' Chlaidheimh* blew open at a sudden gust of sea breeze.

We both gazed at the book.

Among the broken filaments of its wrapping, the pages began to move in the eerie wind that whistled down the stairs, ruffling with an impatient hand looking for a particular or passage.

I began to shiver. My skin felt cold, clammy. My stomach heaved, but I managed to swallow the sickness down. Black spots danced in front of my eyes.

From a distance I heard Basil say, "I told you, you weren't ready for true book hunting." He was sweating despite the chill, wet air, and the whites of his eyes shone overbrightly in the dimming light. *Was* the light dimming, or was that me? I wiped hastily at my eyes.

The ground suddenly jumped as though beneath an aftershock.

I lowered my hand. "What in the name of All was that?" I asked faintly.

"I told you, but you wouldn't listen." Basil was talking rapidly. "I didn't want this. I don't like you, but I didn't want this. But you leave me no choice —"

I couldn't tear my gaze from the *Faileas a' Chlaidheimh.* The pages had stopped turning. I looked down at a hand-painted picture of a strange creature — a cross between a water snake and a dragon. Silver scales and a gray crest.

"...about selling the book and taking it to dealers who —"

"Basil." I broke off as the earth shook again. "*Basil* —" It took effort to get onto my knees. The pain, hard on the heels of the initial numbness, was astounding. I could feel the slick warmth of my blood spilling over my cold skin, soaking my shirt and jacket. It seemed like a great deal of blood. Of course, it always does when it's your own.

I raised my head, and Basil was pointing the revolver at me again. I said desperately, "Don't you know what that is?"

"Shut up."

"Basil —"

Another voice, louder than mine, cried, “Basil, stop!” Irania Briggs appeared in the doorway. “Are you *mad*? What are you doing?”

“I told you to leave this to me.”

“And I told you this would not be necessary.”

“You don’t know what you’re talking about,” he snarled. “Anstruther won’t care how we get the book, so long as we get it.”

“Anstruther is *dead*. He died last night. Lavenham rang me up a few hours ago.”

“All the better,” he said wildly. “Then we can sell the book to the highest bidder!”

“Don’t be stupid. If you kill Bliss, Marx will have both our heads.”

I wondered if she meant that literally. There was a great deal I didn’t know about the Vox Pessimires — and would apparently never learn now. I pressed my fingers hard against the pulse of blood. My shoulder throbbed in painful answer to the pressure.

“If you’ve lost your nerve —”

“Lost *my* nerve?” Irania sounded disbelieving. “I haven’t lost my nerve. You’ve lost your mind.”

“I always knew this partnership was a mistake.” Basil swung the pistol toward Irania. It might have simply been the direction he was moving, but I can’t say I blamed her when she stepped aside and drew her own weapon. She shot him point-blank. The blast seemed to reverberate on and on, bouncing off the stone walls and ceiling.

Basil dropped his revolver, which hit the flagstones with a clatter. He fell beside the grimoire. Blood spread beneath him like a lake of fire. I edged away from the red tide, my muscles quivering with the effort of movement. More than anything I wanted to lie down and close my eyes. Things were moving at such a rate, I couldn't seem to comprehend…

"Bloody fool." Irania stepped into the cell, her pistol still pointed at Basil, but his eyes were fixed and unmoving on the opposite wall. She kicked his gun away, stooped, hefted the *Faileas a' Chlaidheimh* into her arms. She hastily wiped the blood at the edges of it on her skirt.

The earth gave another sharp jump beneath us. The lantern light flickered.

"Do you know what that is?" I said to her.

"I know." She spared me a glance, added conversationally, "You should have joined me when you had the chance."

"You have to put that back. It's the only chance for any of us."

"It's far too late for that, unfortunately." She moved to the archway, turning back to me to add, "I wouldn't linger here if I were you."

I saw a shadow move on the stairs behind her. Numbly I watched her turn and walk into whoever waited there. Irania gave a squeal that did not quite fit with her hardened-lady-adventurer image, but recovered quickly, reaching for her pistol once more. In this, she was thwarted. The gun and book both were wrested from her, and she was sent stumbling back into the cell. Septimus was right behind her.

He looked at Basil's motionless form without a flicker of emotion. His gaze moved on to me. The lines of his face tightened. He looked very angry — as angry as he ever allowed himself to look.

"How badly are you hurt?"

"It could be worse, I think."

Septimus seemed to experience some inward struggle before he stepped over Basil's corpse and dropped to one knee beside me.

"In the name of All, why did you try to do this alone? Why didn't you wake me?"

"I don't know. I didn't want to drag you into it any further if I could help it."

He looked at me like I was an idiot — which I suppose I was — before pulling my hand away from the wound. He swallowed hard.

"On the bright side, you won't have to do it," I offered. It wasn't logical, but somehow, even if I was dying, I felt immeasurably better with Septimus there.

"You're not going to die!"

"We're all going to die if we don't get out of here," Irania said from the other side of the cell.

As though to confirm her words, the lantern went out, and the cell plunged into stygian darkness. A terrible, unearthly cry rent the night. It sounded like a million centurion trumpets echoing through the highest and coldest mountains. It was…indescribable. I clutched at Septimus. It took a second or two, but then he gripped me back with equal fervor.

Just for an instant. Then he said, his voice muffled against my ear, "Stay here. I'll come back for you. I swear it."

The next moment he was gone.

I closed my eyes. Good. Let Septimus deal with it. If anyone could fix this, it would be he.

The earth shook again, and that harrowing cry seemed to sunder the sky. I expected the chapel to cave in on us.

On me. Because I was now alone. Unless I wished to include Basil's body and the mummified remains of the ancient sorceress. It occurred to me that if I was going to die, I didn't want to do it down here. I'd prefer to be with Septimus. Or as near as I could get. He was bound to need help, and unluckily for him, I was the closest thing to it.

I pushed up, clinging weakly to the damp wall as I dragged myself to my feet. Feeling my way across the stone floor, I stepped in something slick and sticky that might have been Basil's blood or might have been my own.

I didn't think I would make it up the stairs or down the aisle and out of the church. With every step, I felt certain I had gone as far as I could go, but somehow I kept moving, one foot in front of the other. I was well beyond pain by then. It had come down to sheer willpower. I was simply determined that nothing was going to keep me from following Septimus.

The first thing I saw when I pushed out through the chapel doors was that the tall trees were on fire. Their brilliance against the night blinded me at first. Then I saw a gray form moving against the backdrop of sky and stars, something vast and swaying. I thought — I have no idea why — that it must be a tornado, because a powerful wind was blowing, bending the burning trees in half and sending statues toppling.

Then I saw two red stars burning high in the sky — and I realized that these were the eyes of the Cirein-cròin.

The wind — the fish-stinking, hot blast of the monster's breath — knocked me down. I wondered if I would catch on fire too, and I curled against the side of the building, scanning the darkness for Septimus.

Faintly, as though from miles and miles away, I heard a voice.

Wildly I looked around, and I saw Septimus standing where the elegant tunnel of trees had once stood. He held the *Faileas a' Chlaidheimh* open, and he was reading from it.

I couldn't hear the words over the howling wind and the creaking and groaning of the chapel, which sounded like it was ready to tear out of its foundation and blow away.

Septimus's black hair whipped around his face. He took a step back as the wind seemed to pummel him. He bent his head lower and continued to read. I could see his lips moving. He never looked up but turned the next page of the grimoire.

The earth seemed to shudder and drop. Suddenly the wind stopped.

All sound stopped.

The sky was empty. The world was silent.

Very distantly I could hear Septimus's voice — a hoarse thread — and then it died out.

I opened my eyes at a drop of moisture. It was raining. A silvery, fine mist wafted through the air like a veil.

Across the clearing, Septimus closed the grimoire. He shut his eyes, seemed to sway and then steady. He turned toward the chapel and saw me trying to get to my feet. He came and made me sit down again.

I gasped, "Is it over?"

He nodded, swiftly unbuttoning his shirt. "I told you to stay put. Why will you never listen to me?"

"That…wasn't a reasonable…request."

He shrugged out of his shirt and began to tear it, with eye-opening strength, into rags. "You've lost the devil of a lot of blood, Colin."

"It's all right."

"It is?" He spared me an exasperated look.

"It's better than…" I stopped. It didn't seem like a wise idea to remind him he was supposed to kill me. He must have read me, though, because he said, "You're going to drive me mad. I tried to tell you last night. The situation is entirely changed."

"How?"

"If you would only trust me…"

He sounded more troubled than impatient. I said quickly, "I do." This was followed by a yelp as he began to tie the strips of his shirt in a rough but efficient bandage about my shoulder. "Not as a nurse, however!"

"Just hold still." I think he tried to be gentle, but it hurt all the same. I listened distantly as he said, "It's different, because for some reason I don't understand, the fey wished you to find the *Faileas a' Chlaidheimh*. A member of the Seelie Court *helped* you. You had their blessing in this quest of yours. It's Old Magick. The oldest. And whatever else it means" — he took a steadying breath — "you're safe now."

It seemed too much to take in after all that had happened. "What next?" I tried to read his face. He was white with weariness.

"We have to put the book back."

"Back?"

He nodded.

"But won't someone else find it?"

"No. The word will spread that the *Faileas a' Chlaidheimh* was destroyed by the Vox Pessimires."

"But what if the Cirein-cròin comes back?"

"It won't," Septimus said grimly.

"But…but what if it does?"

"Then we'll deal with the threat then. The book is too dangerous. No one can be trusted with it." His eyes met mine, and they were greener that the ocean that was now materializing in the pallid dawn. “If you were dying, I would use the book to try to bring you back. Now do you understand?”

“Well, to be honest, I would sort of hope you would.”

He stared at me and started to laugh. At last he wiped tears from the corners of his eyes. “I do love you,” he said. “You’re a bloody primitive, but I’ve never loved anyone as much.”

“That’s fine. I’m getting rather fond of you too. Especially if you’re not going to try to kill me.”

It had to be exhaustion and relief from strain that had him laughing unsteadily again. I couldn’t tell if it was tears or rain streaking his colorless face.

* * * * *

Sodden ash and graying embers drifted down as we walked slowly back to the chapel. Septimus left me sitting in a pew and went through the gilt gate. I heard his footsteps echo as he hurried down the stairway. I stared at the grim statue of Agro Urquhart and made myself rise and follow Septimus down to the chamber.

I leaned against the archway, watching him clean up the grisly remains of the night. First the grimoire went into the tomb, then Basil’s body, then Swanhild’s.

“Did you see what happened to Irania?” I asked suddenly, looking around as though she might still be lurking.

Septimus shook his head. He didn’t seem particularly worried.

“She knows where I found the *Faileas a’ Chlaidheimh*. She might come after it again.”

"No. She'll never believe you returned it to the same resting place."

Perhaps he had a point. *I* had trouble believing we were doing so.

He knocked the chocks away, one by one, so that the lid settled down by regular degrees. When only one wedge remained, Septimus thrust the spikes and two crowbars inside. He hammered at the final wedge. It yielded; the lid swooped down and crashed into place.

He piled the rubble behind the tomb, gathered our tools and lantern.

We stared for a few moments at the puddle of Basil's blood. Our eyes met, but what was there to say?

When we stepped out of the chapel for the last time, the damp morning air was astonishingly cool and fresh. It felt like days had passed rather than a few hours since I had made my way through the darkness to this place. The rain had put out most of the fires, though a few trees still smoldered as we made our way through the overgrowth. It was hard going even with Septimus's help.

In the middle of the bridge to the large island, we stopped, and Septimus threw the mallet as far as he could. It spun through the silvery air and vanished with a splash into the churning green water below.

Septimus put his arm around me once more, and I leaned gratefully into his strength. We continued across the bridge. All at once I heard that eerie moaning I'd heard once before drifting up through the cool, salty air.

I looked at Septimus. "What is that sound?"

He smiled wearily. "The seals are singing."

"What are they singing about?"

The lines of his face softened. He drew me closer. "New beginnings."

ABOUT THE AUTHOR

A distinct voice in gay fiction, multi-award-winning author JOSH LANYON has been writing gay mystery, adventure and romance for over a decade. In addition to numerous short stories, novellas, and novels, Josh is the author of the critically acclaimed Adrien English series, including The Hell You Say, winner of the 2006 USABookNews awards for GLBT Fiction. Josh is an Eppie Award winner and a three-time Lambda Literary Award finalist.

Find other Josh Lanyon titles at www.josh.lanyon.com

Made in the USA
Lexington, KY
18 August 2012